WHITE LIES

John started the engine and backed up, keeping Rick Andover's Camaro in sight.

In the glare of the streetlights, Elizabeth studied John's face. His jaw was set, and he looked fiercely determined. Feeling disturbed, she stared through the windshield at Rick Andover's taillights. She couldn't help wishing she and John weren't doing this.

"He's pulling over," she spoke up moments later.

John nodded and slowed. Then he carefully pulled up to the curb behind another car. He and Elizabeth watched as Rick casually looked left and right, then sauntered across the street. His dark hair cast a shadow on his face and made him look sinister and furtive.

With a jolt Elizabeth realized Rick was heading for the Mello Music Shop, where he worked. A streetlight illuminated the front of the shop, spotlighting a drum set, an amplifier, and a gleaming electric guitar. Rick disappeared into the alley beside the shop. John and Elizabeth waited in tense silence.

Suddenly, a fleeting, stealthy movement in the darkness caught Elizabeth's eye.

"John!" Elizabeth grabbed his arm. While they watched, the electric guitar rose up and disappeared into the black emptiness of the shop. A patch of light outlined a hand gripping the neck of the guitar before it vanished.

"He's stealing it," she breathed, her heart pounding. She turned to John. "He's robbing the store!"

Bantam Books in the Sweet Valley High Series
Ask your bookseller for the books you have missed

SWEET VALLEY HIGH

WHITE LIES

Written by
Kate William

Created by
FRANCINE PASCAL

BANTAM BOOKS
TORONTO · NEW YORK · LONDON · SYDNEY · AUCKLAND

RL 6, IL age 12 and up

WHITE LIES
A Bantam Book / February 1989

Sweet Valley High is a registered trademark of Francine Pascal.

Conceived by Francine Pascal.

Produced by Daniel Weiss Associates, Inc.,
27 West 20th Street,
New York, NY 10011

Cover art by James Mathewuse

ISBN 0-553-27720-0

Published simultaneously in the United States and Canada

Bantam Books are published by Bantam Books, a division of Bantam Doubleday Dell Publishing Group, Inc. Its trademark, consisting of the words "Bantam Books" and the portrayal of a rooster, is Registered in U.S. Patent and Trademark Office and in other countries. Marca Registrada. Bantam Books, 666 Fifth Avenue, New York, New York 10103.

PRINTED IN THE UNITED STATES OF AMERICA

O   0 9 8 7 6 5 4 3 2 1

WHITE LIES

One

Elizabeth Wakefield removed the cover from a typewriter in the *Oracle* office and sat down, deep in thought. Writing her weekly column for Sweet Valley High's student newspaper was a constant challenge, but one she enjoyed. She frowned slightly as she rolled a sheet of paper into the typewriter. Then she began tapping out the latest installment of "Eyes and Ears."

Even though it was officially a gossip column, "Eyes and Ears" was never spiteful or malicious. Elizabeth always kept it lighthearted, and as a rule, most people were thrilled to be featured in it. Elizabeth's blue-green eyes sparkled with amusement as she typed.

Just as she sat back to reread her work, the door to the *Oracle* office burst open.

"Liz! There you are!" Jessica Wakefield rushed in like a cyclone. "You've got to say yes, Liz,"

Jessica cried dramatically. "Please, please, please say yes!"

Elizabeth gave her identical twin sister a skeptical look. "What exactly am I supposed to be agreeing to? Holding up a bank? Giving you all my worldly goods?"

"Oh, come on, Liz!" A splutter of laughter escaped from Jessica as she perched on the edge of a desk and dropped her pink duffel bag onto the floor. Tossing back her spun-gold hair, Jessica added, "Would I ask that?"

For a moment Elizabeth was tempted to answer with a deafening *yes*. With Jessica, everything was absolutely urgent, whether it was wearing the perfect outfit or waiting to make a grand entrance at a party. And sometimes little details got overlooked, like whose clothes she was wearing or who she was causing to wait for her. She was tempestuous and exciting, a self-centered five-foot-six whirlwind.

And the most amazing thing about Jessica was that she was Elizabeth's identical twin. Superficially, the two girls looked like carbon copies. Both of them shared the same tan-California-girl beauty, the same sunny blond hair and perfect size-six figure. Right down to their identical gold lavalieres and the dimples in each girl's left cheek, the Wakefield twins were mirror images of each other. But that's where the resemblance ended.

2

While Jessica was flighty and inconsistent, Elizabeth was steady and thoughtful. She enjoyed reading, thinking, talking with her close friends, and doing things with her boyfriend, Jeffrey French. People instinctively knew that Elizabeth was a sympathetic friend, and everyone turned to her for advice. By contrast, Jessica was known to be interested in only one person—herself.

But in spite of their differences, Elizabeth and Jessica had a special bond that no one else could understand. Elizabeth knew her twin better than anyone else ever would, and despite the trouble Jessica sometimes caused, Elizabeth was fiercely loyal to her twin.

"OK, what is it?" Elizabeth asked, heaving a deep sigh.

Jessica smiled angelically. "It's just one *tiny* favor, Liz. Mom asked me to do some laundry this afternoon, but A.J. and I are dying to go to the Dairi Burger—and everyone's going, so it's almost like I *have* to go. Mom'll kill me if it isn't done by dinner, so could you do it for me, please?" she asked in a rush, her eyes wide and appealing.

Elizabeth remained silent. The twins' mother, Alice Wakefield, worked full-time as an interior designer, so the twins were responsible for many of the household chores. Somehow, though, Jessica managed to wriggle out of at least one obligation a week. And it was usually Elizabeth who took up the slack.

"Liz?" Jessica began to look worried. "Lizzie? I know I've asked you for millions of favors, but this time I'll do something incredibly great to pay you back. Really. *Honest*. I just *have* to go."

The panic in Jessica's voice finally got to Elizabeth. She let out a dry chuckle and nodded. "OK, OK. I don't want to deprive you of something so crucial," she said, giving her twin a knowing look. The truth was, Jessica and her friends went to the Dairi Burger almost every day. But who was counting? Jessica beamed at her happily, and Elizabeth added, "Maybe later you could hand-wash that silk sweater of mine you borrowed."

"Sure, Liz, whatever." Jessica had already jumped off the desk and was heading for the door. "See you later," she sang out as she rushed from the office.

There was a stumbling sound out in the hall, and Elizabeth heard her twin giggle an apology. Then John Pfeifer, the *Oracle*'s sports editor, came in, grappling with an armload of books.

"Just had a head-on collision?" Elizabeth asked, her eyes twinkling.

John nodded and gave her an absent smile while he dumped his books in a slithering heap on a table.

"That's Jessica," Elizabeth said. "She doesn't

4

exactly look before she leaps." Jessica was always in a hurry to do something, and lately everything she did involved her new boyfriend, A. J. Morgan. They had been together for some weeks, a record for Jessica, Elizabeth reflected. The relationship had gotten off to a rocky start, due to a tangle of misunderstandings and one of Jessica's legendary plans. But now the two were inseparable. And as much as Elizabeth hated to admit it, she was a little surprised at how long the romance had lasted. But she was happy for her twin.

She turned back to her typewriter to add a few final lines to her column. When she had finished, she glanced over at John. He was sitting hunched over a handful of papers, scowling.

"What's up?" she asked.

John didn't say anything. "John?"

He jumped slightly and looked up. "Sorry. What?"

"I just said what's up? Is everything all right?" she prodded gently.

"Oh. Sure—I'm just writing up the varsity soccer game, that's all," he replied. With an obvious effort at sounding casual, he added, "Jeffrey had a great game."

Elizabeth's boyfriend was one of the team's starters, and lately his playing had been brilliant.

Elizabeth smiled politely, but she was concerned by John's moodiness. Usually he was

5

one of the most cheerful, easygoing guys at school. Lately, though, he had seemed introspective and withdrawn. She couldn't help feeling sympathetic toward John, because working together for so long on the newspaper had made them good friends.

"Are you sure something isn't—I don't know— getting you down?" Elizabeth asked. "I mean, I don't want to be nosy, but you seem kind of depressed."

John let out a long sigh and hitched his chair closer to the desk. Biting his lower lip, he drummed his pencil against one palm and stared at his newspaper article. He nodded, then looked up at Elizabeth.

"I don't know—it's just—" He frowned. "It's just— Do you know Jennifer Mitchell?"

Elizabeth pictured the pretty sophomore and nodded. "I don't know her well, but I know who she is." Jennifer's long, straight blond hair and cleft chin made her attractive in an unusual but memorable way.

"See—our families have been friends for ages and, well . . ." A warm blush swept across his face, finishing his sentence for him without words.

"I know," Elizabeth offered, smiling warmly. "You think she's pretty special, I guess."

He gave her a lopsided grin and shrugged. "Yeah."

Their eyes met, and a look of understanding

passed between them. "So why are you so down?" Elizabeth asked.

The grin faded from John's face. He folded his arms across his chest and slumped in his chair. "Well, she doesn't exactly feel the same way, but that's not even the real problem," he added hastily. His expression was troubled while he continued. "See, she's started hanging around with Rick Andover. He's the first guy she's ever really gone out with, and she talks about him all the time. She really thinks he's cool."

Elizabeth stared at John with pity. If it were just a case of jealousy, that would be one thing. But she knew perfectly well why John was so concerned with the situation: Rick Andover was trouble. Serious trouble.

In fact, Rick Andover almost ruined Elizabeth's own reputation at one point. It all started with Jessica, naturally. The handsome, dark-haired dropout was definitely attractive—in a dangerous kind of way—and Jessica had fallen for him hard. When Jessica was brought home by the police after Rick got into a fight at a sleazy bar, rumor spread that it was Elizabeth going out with him, and people started giving her the cold shoulder. Of course, the whole mess was eventually straightened out, but ever since then, every time Elizabeth heard about some exploit or scrape with the law involving Rick Andover, she had to repress a shudder. So if the girl John Pfeifer cared about was head over heels in love with Rick, Elizabeth could only feel sorry for John.

"That's—that's terrible," she said lamely. At the moment she didn't know what else to say.

John rolled his eyes. "Yeah, and it's practically all my fault, too," he muttered. When Elizabeth looked surprised, he explained. "See, she plays the piano, electric keyboards and stuff. I drove her to the Mello Music Shop to look at sheet music a couple of weeks ago, and *he* works there. They started talking, and he acted like she was the hottest thing to hit music since Elvis Presley."

"That's his style, I guess," Elizabeth said. She shook her head as she looked at him. "But doesn't she know he has a really bad reputation? I mean, he's been arrested before," she added on a note of concern.

John made an impatient gesture with one hand. "Drunk driving, brawling, vandalism—she knows it all, thanks to her father. He's a lawyer—you know, at Wells and Wells?" Elizabeth nodded and he went on. "So anyway, Mr. Mitchell sometimes volunteers legal help down at Juvenile Hall, so he's seen Rick's whole sheet."

"But Jennifer doesn't care?" Elizabeth pushed. "Doesn't she realize . . . ?"

He met her eyes squarely. "She thinks he gets in trouble because he's lonely and deprived.

8

He gave her this long sob story about his unhappy childhood. I don't know. She feels sorry for him, I guess."

Elizabeth bit back a sarcastic reply because she knew John really needed a friendly ear. Privately, though, she had to think that Jennifer was a pretty bad judge of character to fall for a guy like Rick. But if John liked her, she had no business criticizing the girl. And besides, John looked completely miserable.

"I mean, I don't get it," he exploded suddenly. "How can she like the guy? He's bad news and a total loser!" John's green eyes were filled with hurt and anger, and he smacked his pencil down on the desk vehemently.

Elizabeth hazarded a guess. "Well, maybe she thinks she can help him." She gave John a doubtful look. "I mean, I know some girls think they can change a guy. You know, reform him."

"*He'll* never change," John scoffed.

Shrugging, Elizabeth added, "I'm not saying I would feel that way, but I know that that's attractive sometimes."

John curled his lip. "That's sick." His tone wasn't as harsh as his words, however. He sounded more upset and sad than outraged.

Elizabeth met his eyes again and shook her head helplessly. "I don't know what else to tell you."

"It's just wrong, that's all I'm saying. And it

burns me up that she can't see what he's really like," John continued. He ran one hand through his wavy hair and sighed. "If she wasn't so naive, he'd never get away with it, you know? Why did she have to choose him for a first boyfriend? I just wish I could straighten her out, that's all."

"Well, it doesn't sound like she wants to be straightened out," Elizabeth said gently. "But, who knows, maybe she'll just open her eyes one day and realize Rick's a phony. And when she opens her eyes, she'll also see you," she added with a coaxing smile.

John shrugged self-consciously. "I don't know . . ."

Elizabeth looked at him silently for a moment, wishing she could make everything better. She knew how it felt to see someone you cared for making big mistakes—she watched her twin make gigantic mistakes all the time. But in her experience there wasn't anything to be done about it. Most times people had to find out for themselves what they were doing wrong. Telling someone what to do rarely did any good, and it often led to even more trouble.

"Listen, all you can do is be a friend to her," Elizabeth suggested. John met her eyes and then looked away. "Really—just stick by her and be there for her when she needs help."

John was silent for a moment, staring off across the newspaper office. "That's the problem. I get the feeling when she needs my help, it'll be because Rick Andover's gotten her into major trouble."

"Oh, come on," Elizabeth said with an attempt at lightness. But she secretly thought the sports editor was right.

John shook his head stubbornly and set his jaw. "I'm just afraid of what could happen. Knowing that guy, it could really be bad news."

Two

Jessica blew on the back of A.J.'s neck while he tried for bonus points on the pinball machine. A lazy smile curled up the sides of her mouth as she tried to break his concentration. She tugged on a lock of his wavy red hair.

"A.J.," she crooned, her mouth close to his ear. Her vivid blue-green eyes sparkled mischievously.

"Yeah?" A.J. didn't take his eyes off the machine, and a frown of intense absorption wrinkled his forehead.

"Aaaay-Jaaaay," she whispered.

Throwing her a lopsided grin, A.J. shook his head and released another ball. "It won't work, Wakefield," he teased, matching her look.

Jessica giggled. "I don't know what you're talking about."

"Yeah. Right."

Jessica smiled and looked at A.J.'s profile. She loved his lean, chiseled jawline and the serious, thoughtful expression in his brown eyes. He could be quiet and studious, and he loved poetry, but he could also beat the best player at pinball, too. Jessica tried again to distract him by lightly rubbing his arm.

Without taking his eyes off the pinball machine, A.J. drawled, "Forget it. *Yes!*" He interrupted himself with a whoop of triumph. "Two hundred thousand!"

Jessica shrieked and wrapped her arms around him in a tight hug. "Finally. *Now* can we sit down?" she asked, smiling up at him.

"Don't I get a victory kiss?" A.J. raised his eyebrows a fraction, waiting.

Jessica's heart flip-flopped with excitement. Even though they had been dating for weeks, A.J. still had a magical effect on her. Rising on her toes, she placed a seductive kiss on his mouth. From a nearby booth a round of applause and whistles went up.

"Hey, no public displays of you-know-what!" called out Winston Egbert, the junior class-clown.

"Yeah," joined in Tom McKay. "You might start a riot."

Jessica and A.J. smiled innocently and went to stand in line for sodas. They brought them back to the crowded booth where their friends were sitting and squeezed in beside them. There was a brief, chaotic reshuffling. Lila Fowler and Cara Walker, Jessica's two best friends, were across the booth from her. Wedged into the corners were Neil Freemount and Dana Larson, and Ken Matthews straddled a chair and propped his elbows on the Formica tabletop. Maria Santelli was precariously sharing a chair with Winston, her boyfriend.

"So, is everyone coming to my party on Friday?" Dana asked the group. Dana was a tall, leggy blond, the lead singer for The Droids, the school's most popular band.

A wide smile broke over Jessica's face. Parties were the highlight of her life. "Are you kidding? Absolutely."

Beside her, A.J. stirred in his seat and nudged her elbow. "Jessica, remember? We're supposed to go up to my uncle's for dinner Friday."

"But—" She felt a sting of irritation and took a long gulp of her soda to stall for time. She hated to be contradicted. And she wanted to go to Dana's party. Forcing a bright smile, she said, "We can go after dinner."

A.J. looked concerned. He lowered his voice a notch. "But, Jessica, it's a two-hour drive. We'd have to leave too early."

Across the table, Lila sent Jessica a questioning glance. Jessica kept smiling, but her tone was firm. "Well, how long did you plan on staying, anyway?" she asked. Arguing in front

14

of their friends was something she didn't want to do, but she had to get things settled.

"Well, at least till nine or ten," A.J. replied.

"But then we wouldn't even—"

"Oo-hoo! What's this? A little lovers' quarrel?" Winston cut in. He grinned and darted his eyes back and forth between them. The others around the table began teasing, too.

"Don't let her boss you around, A.J.," Ken warned.

"Stick up for your rights, Jess," put in Maria.

Jessica felt a blush of embarrassment sweep over her cheeks, but when she looked up at A.J., she saw the good-natured acceptance in his eyes. She smiled. "Let's talk about it later, OK?"

"Good idea," he agreed, shaking his head and laughing. "In private."

Sighing, Jessica took another sip of her soda and let her eyes roam around the crowded hamburger restaurant. The door opened, and a figure caught her eye. "Oh, gross." She shuddered.

"What? Who is it?" Cara said, craning around.

Jessica rolled her eyes and watched the tall, dark-haired boy cross the Dairi Burger. "Rick Andover—scum de la scum."

"Oh, you're kidding."

A.J. looked mildly surprised. "What's wrong with the guy?"

"Well . . ." Jessica and Cara and Lila ex-

15

changed a significant look. Then Jessica explained. "He's a total loser, that's his problem. First he dropped out of school and just cruised around all the time—"

"As if that were really impressive," Lila put in disdainfully.

Jessica nodded. "Right. So then he started telling everybody how he'd got this great music career all lined up—how he was going to L.A. to play for some big record companies and agents and stuff."

"So what happened?" A.J. prompted. He sat back in the booth and folded his arms.

Dana Larson leaned forward, her brown eyes filled with scorn. "Nothing. And it was *always* someone else's fault, according to him. He always made it sound like people were jealous of him and that they'd sabotaged his big chance."

"So he didn't exactly become a big rock star," A.J. concluded wryly.

"Not even close."

"Hey, Dana," Winston put in. "Didn't he try to join The Droids?"

Dana shrugged and ran one hand through her short blond hair. "He tried, but first of all, he had no talent on the guitar, and second, he was a total goof-off. He wouldn't come to rehearsals, and he got high all the time. He wanted all the good stuff and none of the work."

"I hate guys like that," A.J. said. He shook his head. "What a pain."

"No kidding," Dana replied. "He's a total farce."

Ken spoke up. "You know he works at Mello Music. Every time you go in there he tries to tell you about his big break in L.A. and how everyone was out to ambush him because he's so good."

A.J. snorted. "He sounds like a pretty paranoid guy."

"No. He's just a fool," Jessica corrected him.

She watched while Rick Andover left the cashier, tray in hand, and joined Jennifer Mitchell at a booth. The girl's face lit up with a brilliant smile as he spoke to her, and Jessica repressed a sneer. Obviously Jennifer was head over heels in love.

"*She* must be an even bigger fool," Jessica said. "What does she see in him?"

Lila giggled softly. "Same thing you saw maybe?" she said in an undertone.

Jessica sent her friend a fierce warning look and glanced at A.J. to see if he had heard Lila. Jessica didn't particularly want him to know she had once dated Rick Andover herself. But he was still listening to Dana and the others and seemed not to have noticed.

Jessica turned back to her friends.

"Jennifer could be good if she really tried,"

Dana observed to the group. She was looking speculatively at Rick Andover and Jennifer Mitchell, too.

"Good at what?" Cara asked.

Dana rattled ice in the bottom of her cup. "Keyboards—piano, synthesizers—but I don't know if she's got the drive. She might, with the right group. I heard her one afternoon, when she was just goofing on the piano in the band room, and she wasn't bad at all."

Jessica shrugged. She couldn't be bothered about someone who was dating Rick Andover.

"Ready to go?" A.J. asked, a warm, open smile on his face.

Pushing herself up, Jessica nodded emphatically. "Definitely. Let's hit the road. Catch you later, everyone."

On the way home Jessica brought up the subject of Dana's party again. "You've never been to one of Dana's parties before, so you don't know. She gives the best parties."

A.J.'s expression was stubborn as he turned up the Wakefields' street. "I promised my uncle we'd come though."

"I know, A.J." Jessica decided it was time to turn on the charm. She slid closer to him and took his hand. "And I really want to meet your grandfather, too," she murmured, giving A.J. a melting look. She laced her fingers with his. "But it's really important to me. All our friends will be there. And we could have dinner with him some other time, right?"

"Well . . ."

"I mean, it doesn't have to be *this* Friday, does it?" she continued.

The car rolled to a stop in front of the Wakefields' attractive split-level house. A.J. turned off the ignition and sat staring straight ahead. "I don't know. I'd hate to cancel on him."

Jessica resisted the urge to scream. Why did A.J. always have to be so conscientious? She slid her arms around his neck and put her cheek against his. "Please, A.J. Just this once." She felt him tighten his arms around her. "Please."

"All right." He sighed and let out a soft chuckle. "You got me."

"You're great, A.J. You're really great," Jessica murmured. She sat up and met his gaze evenly. Then she leaned forward and gave him a long, lingering kiss. She opened the car door. "I'll see you tomorrow," she said with a dazzling smile.

"OK. Bye."

As A.J. drove off, Jessica hugged herself happily. Nothing was so satisfying as getting her own way. She headed for the front door, deep in thought.

I always thought Liz was crazy for going out with just one boy at a time, she reflected soberly. *But this is turning out just fine.*

*   *   *

Jennifer Mitchell carefully closed the front door behind her and paused to listen. The low murmur of the television drifted out from the living room. Hugging her books to her chest, she hurried silently toward the stairs.

"Is that you, Jen?" Her mother's voice halted her in her tracks.

Jennifer swallowed hard before she answered. She couldn't let her parents know there was anything different or unusual going on. In a calm, steady voice she replied, "Hi, Mom. Sorry I'm late. I—I stopped at the Dairi Burger with some friends."

Without waiting for an answer, she turned and ran up to her room. Breathless, she shut the door and leaned against it, her heart racing.

Across her small bedroom, Jennifer caught sight of herself in the mirror over her bureau. Her brown eyes were sparkling with happiness and excitement. "Rick, I love you so much," she whispered to her reflection. "It's going to be so great."

Her glance fell on her electronic keyboard, and a ripple of fear and excitement ran through her. She crossed the room and switched on the power for the portable keyboard. Her fingers wandered over the keys, striking chords at random. Suddenly she splayed her fingers and made a harsh, discordant sound. She turned away.

"I've got to tell somebody," she muttered, biting her lower lip.

The feelings bottled up inside her were so powerful, so intense, that she couldn't keep still. Every muscle was tensed, ready for action. But Jennifer knew she had to keep herself in check until the right time. Until then, she needed an outlet, someone to confide in.

Her parents were out of the question, of course. If they had any idea what she and Rick were planning, they would have a fit! For some reason they absolutely hated Rick. No one really understood him, Jennifer thought indignantly. Not the way she did. They didn't understand him, so they hated him instead. Her father was always reminding her about all the trouble Rick had been in.

"As if it matters," Jennifer scoffed, throwing herself onto her bed. "I don't care about any of that."

Her long, straight blond hair fanned out on her pillow. For a long, dreamy moment she treasured the memory of how Rick had run his hands through it. No one had ever made her feel as special as Rick did. He had dreams and plans and ideas. He had fire.

That was something her parents would never see. They just couldn't understand him—or her either, anymore. When she was younger, she and her parents had always been very close, and her father had been especially good at knowing what was on her mind and cheering her up.

But lately it seemed that neither one of her parents was being supportive. For the first time Jennifer was really in love. Instead of being happy for her, her parents were acting as though she had committed a major crime. So telling them her news was definitely out of the question.

Abruptly she turned on her side, too agitated to stay in one position. "I've got to tell somebody," she whispered.

She scowled to herself as she ran through a mental list of her friends for someone she could trust with the secret. Then, smiling, she sat up and reached for the phone.

Three

After school on Thursday, Elizabeth took a seat in the bleachers and closed her eyes for a moment, enjoying the sun. When she opened them, she immediately searched for Jeffrey among the running soccer players. As soon as she spotted his tall, athletic figure, she smiled. She loved going to soccer practice to watch him. Sometimes she caught up on homework, and sometimes she just watched the players. Knowing he was there filled her with contentment.

Almost as though he felt her gaze, Jeffrey paused and looked in her direction. He waved, then deftly blocked a pass from Aaron Dallas. On the sidelines, the cheerleaders went through their warm-up drills. Elizabeth opened her math book.

For the next ten minutes, she concentrated on her homework. Then she felt the bleachers vibrate as someone climbed up. She raised her head and saw John Pfeifer.

"Hi, John!" she shouted. She raised her hand to attract his attention. "Come sit with me."

John nodded without much enthusiasm and walked slowly toward her. Elizabeth could see the deep lines of anxiety creasing his forehead.

"Hi," he muttered, sinking down next to her.

Elizabeth felt her smile fade. She had never seen John looking so perturbed, and her heart went out to him. "Working on something for the paper?" she asked softly.

He shrugged. "Yeah. Just a follow-up. I don't know." Sighing, he opened a notebook and stared blankly at some notes.

Elizabeth didn't know what to say. Normally she respected people's feelings and gave them their privacy. Of course, she was always ready and willing to listen if a friend needed to talk. But she sensed that John was deeply troubled and didn't know who to turn to, and that he would keep his feelings bottled up unless someone drew him out.

"John," she began hesitantly. He met her eyes, and she gave him an encouraging smile. "You know you can always talk to me if you're feeling down about anything."

He smiled faintly in return. "Thanks. I know."

"So? You want to talk about it?" she coaxed.

He stared straight ahead for a few seconds, as though debating with himself. Then, unexpectedly, he let out a low groan and dropped his face into his hands. "Liz, what am I going to do? It's driving me nuts!"

Elizabeth bit her lip. "What? What's wrong?"

"Remember what I was telling you the other day?" John looked around edgily and shifted on the hard wooden bleachers.

Elizabeth nodded, thinking of Jennifer Mitchell and Rick Andover. As she took in the expression on John's face, a wave of alarm swept over her. Had Rick gotten Jennifer in some kind of trouble just as John had predicted? A dozen speculations raced through her mind.

"What is it?"

Reluctantly, as though it hurt, John explained. "Last night she called me and said—" He broke off, twisting a pencil between his fingers. "You know, normally I would never blab if someone told me a secret. . . ."

"I know," Elizabeth said. She knew it must be very serious for John to betray a confidence. He was obviously very distraught over whatever Jennifer had told him. "I know—and believe me, I won't tell anyone."

John nodded and swallowed audibly. Looking at his hands, he confessed, "She says she and Rick are going to take off—go to New York and start a band."

For a moment Elizabeth was too shocked to utter a word. She stared at John in disbelief. Finally she said, "You mean she's going to run away? Drop out of school?"

He nodded again, rubbing one hand across his eyes. "You got it," he said bitterly.

"Didn't you try talking her out of it?" Elizabeth asked.

John let out a sharp snort. "Are you serious? I practically went hoarse trying to talk her out of it!"

Elizabeth was stunned. It was hard to believe that anyone would contemplate such a crazy scheme. But apparently Jennifer was serious about going through with it. That was further proof that the girl either had very bad judgment or she was completely blinded by infatuation. And the look of anguish in John's eyes told Elizabeth how much it hurt.

"Maybe her parents—" Elizabeth began.

"Oh, come *on*, Liz! She'd never listen to them." John shook his head mournfully. "Liz, I've got to do something, but I don't know what!"

Elizabeth turned away in confusion and stared blankly at the soccer players running up the field. In the past, she had been asked for advice dozens of times. But knowing what to tell someone didn't seem to get easier with practice. It was so difficult to know what to say.

But I'm the one who pushed him into talking, she told herself silently.

"Liz, you've got to help me," John pleaded, sensing her reluctance. He looked at her with sorrowful eyes. "Jennifer is going to ruin her whole life unless I can do something!"

She nodded. All she could do was say what was in her heart. "John, I don't know if this makes any sense, but I think if you tell on her, Jennifer will end up hating you. She'll blame you, and she'll never realize what a mistake it was listening to Rick." Elizabeth looked up quickly to see if her message was getting through.

John was silent, clenching his jaw stubbornly as he looked out across the field. "I can't just ignore it," he finally said angrily.

"No, not exactly," Elizabeth conceded. "But you've got to let Jennifer make her own mistakes. I mean—" She broke off, searching desperately for the right words. "You can't try to control a person's life, even if it's for a good reason. You can't protect Jennifer from herself."

"So I do nothing?" John choked out fiercely. He turned to her, and there was a bleak expression in his eyes. "Just let her go ahead and totally ruin her life?"

Elizabeth shrugged in sympathy. She knew she would have trouble following her own advice if it was someone she cared about.

"Maybe Jennifer will realize what Rick's really like before it's too late. You've got to trust her, you know. But if she's going to go, there's no way you can stop her." She put one hand on his arm. "But if you turn her in, she'll never forgive you. You'll end up losing her friendship for sure."

"Oh, man." John let out a heavy sigh and nodded grudgingly. "I guess you're right. But it just kills me."

"I know," Elizabeth replied, her voice compassionate. "I'm sorry."

"Well, I'll tell you one thing: I'm definitely not going to turn my back on this!" he exploded, his anger returning. "I don't trust Rick Andover for a second, and I'm watching him from now on. If he does anything that isn't a hundred percent legit, I'm going to pin that guy to the wall. I'm not letting him drag Jennifer down with him."

"Good idea," Elizabeth agreed, moved by John's loyalty. "Just be careful."

"I will," John said. "But I'll make sure she sees who's screwing up her life. And it won't be me."

On the sidelines of the soccer field, Jessica collapsed dramatically onto the grass, and Amy Sutton and Cara sprawled next to her.

"I'm totally wiped out," Jessica announced with a weary groan.

"Well, who's in charge here, anyway?" Cara complained. "*You're* co-captain of the squad."

"OK, OK. Don't mutiny on me." Jessica rolled over onto one elbow and surveyed the rest of the cheerleaders. The other co-captain, Robin Wilson, was absent that day, so Jessica was completely in control, just the way she liked it. "That's it for today, you guys."

Moans of relief went up from the cheerleaders. Jessica grinned and let out a contented sigh. Then she turned her gaze toward the soccer players.

"Hey, Aaron," she called out as Aaron Dallas paused nearby.

He lifted one hand to wave and cocked his head to one side. "Hey, Jessica. How's it going?"

"Not bad. Not bad."

Aaron's intent gaze followed the soccer ball, and he was off in a flash.

"He has got *really* muscular legs, did you ever notice?" Amy drawled, tossing back her blond hair.

Jessica giggled. "Me? Notice?" Her blue-green eyes danced mischievously as Michael Schmidt ran by. "Hey, Mike! Keep your eye on the ball!"

Startled, Mike spun around to see who was talking to him and missed the ball as it sped by.

He dove frantically to keep it in bounds, and the cheerleaders laughed.

"I said keep your eye on the ball, didn't I?" Jessica teased.

Mike pointed one finger at her and gave a crooked smile. "You can get a penalty for that, Wakefield," he warned her, laughing.

"Uh-oh! Look out!" Jessica's eyes sparkled flirtatiously, and she gave him a dimpled smile. "What kind of penalty?" she challenged.

With a long, appraising look, Michael replied, "I'll think about it and let you know."

"You do that." Jessica grinned as he dodged away after the ball. She loved flirting. It made life so much more interesting. She sat up and crossed her legs at the ankles, enjoying the sunshine.

"Jess—A.J.'s here." Cara's voice broke into her cheerful musings.

Jessica looked up, surprised. A.J. was standing nearby, watching. As their eyes met, he started walking toward her.

"Hi," she piped up.

He stayed standing, his eyes on the soccer team. "What's going on?" he asked casually.

"Nothing." Jessica squinted up at him. Was it her imagination, or did he seem a little ticked off? "Just sitting here," she added in a defensive tone. She wondered how much of her conversation with Michael he had overheard.

A.J. nodded but said nothing.

For a moment Jessica was tempted to say something sarcastic about how he couldn't expect her to ignore half the world's population just because they were dating. But he hadn't actually *said* anything about her flirting, so she decided to just let it drop.

Besides, he looks so gorgeous right now, she thought, looking up at A.J.'s strong face. *I don't want to get into an argument.*

"Ready to go?" A.J. asked.

Jessica hesitated for a moment. Then she gave him one of her brightest smiles. "Definitely. Let's get out of here."

Elizabeth was silent and moody as Jeffrey drove her home after soccer practice. She sat hunched against the door, frowning out the window at the quiet streets and houses of Sweet Valley. She couldn't stop thinking about John Pfeifer. It was clear he wasn't the type who could turn his back on someone in trouble, and Jennifer Mitchell was in trouble. The problem was, Elizabeth was afraid he could do even more damage by trying to straighten things out. She let out a troubled sigh and rubbed her temples.

"You're being pretty quiet," Jeffrey spoke up,

raising his eyebrows in a question. "What's the problem?"

"I don't know." She sighed. "Sometimes I just don't know what to say to people when they have a problem."

He smiled and reached for her hand. "Everyone ends up pouring out their problems to you," he said in a sympathetic voice. Then his tone changed as he went on. "By the way, I have this deep, dark secret that's been bugging me for—"

"Cut it out!" Elizabeth couldn't help laughing when she realized he was teasing her. She gave him a stern, reproving look that dissolved into a smile. "I'm definitely ready for the weekend, I can tell you that."

"Oh—that reminds me." Jeffrey grimaced and pulled the car over to the curb in front of her house. "I can't make it to Dana's party tomorrow night. My aunt and uncle are coming down from Oregon. Sorry."

Elizabeth tried not to let her disappointment show. One thing she had been looking forward to all week was spending Friday night with Jeffrey. "That's OK," she said. "I understand."

"There's no reason why you shouldn't go without me, though," he added quickly. His green eyes were earnest.

But Elizabeth shrugged. "Oh, I don't know if I really feel like partying anyway. Maybe I'll just stay home and write or something. Really, I could use a quiet night," she continued, seeing the guilty look on Jeffrey's face.

"You're sure?"

"Positive." She leaned forward and kissed him tenderly. Then she opened her door and hopped out. "See you in school tomorrow," she called.

She stood on the curb to watch him drive off, and she was still smiling while she waved. But her thoughts had already returned to John Pfeifer and Jennifer Mitchell. The way things were, she doubted whether the problem could be resolved without someone getting hurt.

Four

On Friday evening Elizabeth drove the red Fiat convertible she and her twin shared out to the Valley Mall. Her favorite bookstore was having a half-price sale, and she knew she could get some real bargains. If she couldn't spend the evening with Jeffrey, at least she could find something really good to read. After a blissful half hour of browsing and buying, she headed back home, a heavy bag of books sitting on the passenger seat next to her. She could hardly wait to curl up with a cup of cocoa and the short stories of Ernest Hemingway.

On the drive back, however, the neon sign of the Dairi Burger caught her attention. Suddenly thirsty, she shifted into low gear and pulled into the crowded parking lot. A cold root beer was just what she needed. She walked through the falling dusk toward the brightly lit ham-

34

burger hangout and stepped inside. She took her place at the end of the long line to order. The restaurant was noisy with activity and voices.

"Hey, Liz! Over here!"

Elizabeth turned and saw Ken Matthews waving to her frantically. He was sitting at a booth with John Pfeifer, Sandra Bacon, Manuel Lopez, and Neil Freemount. Sandra, one of the cheerleaders, started waving, too, when she saw Elizabeth, and then Neil and Manuel beckoned as well.

Nodding, Elizabeth paid for her root beer and maneuvered around the crowded tables. It was like fighting against the surf to get through the crowd. "Hi," she said as she sank down into the booth. "This place is mobbed."

"No kidding—we practically had to start a war over this table," Sandra said, laughing.

Neil took a bite of his hamburger and gave Elizabeth an inquisitive look. "Heading to Dana's?"

She grinned and shook her head. "No, I'm not in a real party mood. How about you guys?" Elizabeth darted a searching look at John, but he didn't seem to be following the conversation.

"That's the plan," Sandra replied. She gave her boyfriend, Manuel, a teasing look as she added, "As soon as these guys finish feeding their faces."

"Hey! No fair!" Manuel tried to look indignant, but since he had just taken a huge bite of hamburger, it didn't work. He shrugged and washed it down with soda while the others laughed. "Anyway, I need fuel for Dana's party," he explained.

As the conversation turned to the party, Elizabeth sat back and sipped her root beer. Part of her wished Jeffrey could have been there and that they were all heading over to the party together. But she didn't really regret missing it that much. There would be other parties to go to, she reflected. Skipping this one wouldn't be such a loss. She turned her gaze on John. So far he hadn't said a word.

"What's up, John?" she asked quietly.

He looked up, startled. "Oh. Nothing."

She cocked her head to one side, giving him a sympathetic look. She knew he was probably brooding about Jennifer, and she searched her imagination for some safe topic of conversation, something that might take his mind off the problem. Between them, Neil and Manuel were teasing Sandra, oblivious of Elizabeth's and John's low voices.

"So, when are you doing a story for the paper about our new tennis star?" Elizabeth asked.

He looked blank. "Huh?"

Grinning over the rim of her paper cup, she taunted, "Oh, so you didn't know, yet, huh? Some ace sports editor *you* are."

John managed a smile, but he still seemed to be far away. "Who are you talking about?" he asked absently, picking at the french fries in front of him.

"Kristin Thompson. She's always off at tennis competitions, and I think she works with a coach every day after school. I bet you'd recognize her if you saw her. I don't think she has many friends, though," Elizabeth added. "Probably because she's always practicing and never has time to hang out."

John didn't respond. Elizabeth was concerned about how preoccupied and anxious he looked. Drawing a deep breath, she continued, "I heard someone say she's been winning junior championships for years."

"Oh, yeah? Thompson?" John asked. His effort to sound attentive wasn't succeeding.

Elizabeth pursued the topic. "Does that name mean something?"

John shrugged. "Well, it's just there was a famous tennis player, Elise Thompson, who died in an accident ten or eleven years ago. And Mr. Thompson owns the tennis club in town."

Elizabeth propped her elbow on the table, hoping she could keep distracting him. "Then maybe there's a connection?" she went on eagerly. "It sure would make sense."

"Yeah," John said in a disinterested tone.

He slumped back and scanned the Dairi Burger with anxious eyes.

Her attempt to cheer him up had failed completely, Elizabeth thought. He was so distant, so caught up in worrying about Jennifer, that he was practically a different person. Sighing ruefully, she followed his gaze. Then she sensed him stiffen suddenly. Rick Andover had just walked in.

"John," Elizabeth said in a warning tone. She looked at him to gauge his reaction. He was staring intently at Rick. Elizabeth cleared her throat. *"John."*

"They're leaving tonight," he said in an undertone. His eyes were still fixed on Rick Andover. "This is it."

She gave him a startled glance. "Did Jennifer actually tell you that?"

"No, but I can tell," he muttered, his eyes on Rick. "I'm going to follow him."

"John! Come on, you can't—"

He turned to her quickly. "Liz, I have to. I know he's going to end up hurting her," John insisted. "Can you come with me?"

Elizabeth flinched at the thought. It didn't seem right that John was getting so fanatical about Rick Andover.

"John, I—"

For a long moment they looked at each other, and John pleaded silently with his eyes. Elizabeth could see the depth of his feelings and, in spite of her uneasiness, felt herself giving way. Finally she gave him a reluctant nod.

"OK." She sighed, darting a nervous glance across the Dairi Burger. Rick Andover was talking to some people near the door and looked as if he was getting ready to leave. She glanced at John again and shook her head. "Are you *really* sure you want to do this?"

He nodded fervently and started to rise. "Yes."

"Hey, you leaving?" Neil spoke up. The others were looking at them curiously.

Elizabeth and John exchanged a look, and Elizabeth explained. "There's something we have to do for the paper. We'll see you later." When she turned to John again, he was already crossing the floor. She gave her friends a shrug and a weak smile and turned to catch up with him.

"He just went to the parking lot," John informed her, walking quickly. "Let's go. Leave your car here. I'll drop you off later."

Elizabeth nodded, nearly running to keep up. *What am I doing?* she asked herself. She knew she should try to discourage John, keep him from jumping to conclusions, but something held her back. Knowing Rick Andover as she did, she couldn't help wondering herself if he was heading for some real trouble. So she kept silent and climbed into John's car.

Without a word, John started the engine and

39

backed up, keeping Rick Andover's Camaro in sight. They pulled out onto the street and headed for town. Up ahead, Rick signaled for a turn, and John followed behind.

In the glare of the streetlights, Elizabeth studied John's face. His jaw was set, and lines of fierce determination were etched into his forehead. Elizabeth ached to say something, but she didn't know what. Feeling disturbed, she stared through the windshield at Rick Andover's taillights. She couldn't help wishing she and John weren't doing this.

"He's pulling over," she spoke up moments later.

John nodded and slowed. Then he carefully pulled up to the curb behind another car. He and Elizabeth watched as Rick casually looked left and right, then sauntered across the street. His dark hair cast a shadow on his face and made him look sinister and furtive.

With a jolt, Elizabeth realized Rick was heading for the Mello Music Shop, where he worked. A streetlight illuminated the front window of the shop, spotlighting a drum set, an amplifier, and a gleaming electric guitar. Rick disappeared into the alley beside the shop. John and Elizabeth waited in tense silence.

"What's he doing?" John whispered. He gripped the steering wheel anxiously, his eyes locked on the darkened store. "What's he up to?"

"I don't know. Maybe he left something at work."

"I doubt it," John said. "Something's going on."

"There could be a perfectly good reason," Elizabeth pointed out. She didn't sound very convincing, even to herself. Biting her lip, she glanced back at the empty music store. A fleeting, stealthy movement in the darkness caught her eye.

"John!" Elizabeth grabbed his arm. While they watched, the electric guitar rose up and disappeared into the black emptiness of the shop. A patch of light outlined a hand gripping the neck of the guitar before it vanished.

"He's stealing it," she breathed, her heart pounding. She turned to John. "He's robbing the store!"

John nodded silently.

Elizabeth could feel her heart beating rapidly. Witnessing Rick Andover commit a crime suddenly put a whole new light on things. It wasn't a matter of jealousy between John and Rick anymore. If Rick had robbed the music store, he could get Jennifer in serious trouble. And Elizabeth saw from John's expression that he had already figured that much out.

"There he is."

Rick emerged from the alley again and looked cautiously around. In one hand he held a guitar case. Apparently satisfied that no one was watching, he stepped out onto the sidewalk and began strolling casually along. Elizabeth and John watched him stop at a phone booth and make a call.

"He's calling Jennifer. I know it," John muttered. "He robbed the music store, so they've got to be leaving tonight."

"I think you're right," Elizabeth replied. She twisted her hands together in her lap. "They're probably arranging where to meet."

John nodded, his expression grim. "I knew he'd pull something like this. I knew it. I'm stopping him right now. And then I'm calling the cops."

"Wait." Elizabeth halted John before he reached for the door. Running off and confronting Rick Andover wasn't the best solution, she knew. John looked at her impatiently. "Listen, the best thing to do is call Luke Lander—he owns the store. It's up to him to decide what he wants to do. He might not want Rick arrested."

John let his breath out slowly and watched Rick hang up the phone. John was obviously struggling with his emotions, but he finally relaxed and nodded. "OK. I guess you're right."

"I know I am. If you call the police and it turns out there's a logical explanation, then Jennifer will find out and be furious with you," Elizabeth continued. "Check with Mr. Lander first, and then you'll know."

The two of them shared a worried look as Rick drove off in his car.

Then, hurrying to the same pay phone, John dug in his pocket for some change. Elizabeth flipped through the thin pages of the phone book until she found Luke Lander's number.

"Here it is: 555-1793."

With a determined nod, John punched in the numbers, and Elizabeth watched him anxiously. As far as she could tell, notifying the store owner of what they had seen was all they could do. After that, it was out of their hands.

Five

A few minutes after midnight Jessica and A.J. strolled hand in hand up to the front door of the Wakefield split-level house. She leaned back against the doorframe and looked up into A.J.'s shadowed face. With a slow, sultry smile she said, "Aren't you glad we went to that party instead of your uncle's?"

"Mmm. I guess so," A.J. replied, leaning down to kiss her.

Jessica wrapped her arms around his neck. Going to Dana's party had definitely been better than spending the evening with A.J.'s uncle, she decided. They had danced for hours and sat on the couch together, sometimes the center of attention and sometimes off in their own private world. She sighed blissfully and stepped back a pace.

"Thanks for a wonderful night."

"Hey. No problem," A.J. said, and gave her a long, lingering kiss.

Then he touched her cheek softly and turned to head back to his car. "I'll talk to you tomorrow," A.J. said. "Good night."

Jessica said good night, blew him a kiss, then slipped inside. She ran lightly up the stairs.

"You still up, Lizzie?" Jessica poked her head into her twin's room. Elizabeth was sitting up in bed, writing in her journal.

Elizabeth looked up briefly. "Oh, hi, Jess."

"What a great party," Jessica announced as she invited herself in. She flopped onto the end of the bed and gazed at the ceiling. "You really should've been there."

"I didn't feel like going," Elizabeth replied in an absent tone.

"Liz Wakefield, you just don't know how to party. A.J. and I danced for hours. The Droids have a whole bunch of new songs, you know." Rolling over onto her elbow, Jessica eyed her sister. She thought her twin looked a little depressed. "So what did you do instead?"

Elizabeth hesitated for a moment and folded her journal shut on one finger. "Just went to the mall and then to the Dairi Burger. Nothing interesting."

"Why couldn't Jeffrey go, anyway?" Jessica watched the slight tightening of her twin's mouth. When Elizabeth didn't say anything, she prompted, "Couldn't you make him go?"

45

"He had other plans, Jess," Elizabeth said. "It's not like I'm in charge of his schedule, you know. He had some family obligation."

Jessica let out a snort and rolled her eyes. "Well, so did A.J., but I got him to switch," she said complacently. She toyed with a strand of her hair and went on in a dreamy voice. "He's such a great guy, Liz. He'll do anything for me. Anything I ask."

"Hmm."

"I'm totally serious," Jessica insisted. She gave her twin a sidelong glance, wondering if Elizabeth was jealous of the relationship she and A.J. had. Maybe Elizabeth was irritated because she couldn't get Jeffrey to change his mind and be reasonable. "Listen, you want to hear my philosophy about men?"

Elizabeth gave her a skeptical look. "Not really, but you'll tell me anyway."

"That's right." Pushing herself up off the bed, Jessica sauntered over to the mirror and critically examined her face. "My theory about men is you have to make them do what you want," she explained. She carefully picked off a clump of mascara and flicked it away. "Otherwise, they'll never think of it themselves."

Elizabeth remained silent.

"I mean, for instance, A.J. went and told his uncle we would both have dinner with him tonight, without even realizing I didn't want to," Jessica continued. She hunted for a moment around Elizabeth's bureau and picked up some pearl earrings. As she tried them on in front of the mirror, she added, "So I had to tell him we should go to Dana's instead—obviously."

Elizabeth let out an impatient sigh. "So you're saying I should've done the same thing to Jeffrey—just order him to go to the party? You're crazy, Jess. Never in a million years."

"Liz." Through the mirror, Jessica sent her twin a pitying look and shook her head. "If he really cared, he wouldn't have made you stay home all alone on a Friday night."

"He didn't make—"

"But A.J. and I really have a unique relationship, Liz. I guess you can't help it if your relationship isn't perfect like ours. I bet you never thought we'd last so long, did you?" She turned on her sister suddenly. "*Did* you?"

Elizabeth looked surprised. "I don't know, Jess. I never really—"

"Anyway, I'm so exhausted, Liz. I can't stay up another second. Sorry."

Smiling angelically, Jessica drifted through the adjoining bathroom door. Sometimes it was just impossible to communicate to people how special her relationship with A.J. was. And if she could only get A.J. to change his mind about going to his uncle's the next night, when everyone else would be going to Guido's, everything would be perfect.

47

Sighing, Elizabeth leaned back against her headboard and closed her eyes. The last thing she was in the mood for was listening to her twin babbling on and on about her fabulous romance. Not that Elizabeth wasn't happy her sister was in love, but Jessica's monologues could get pretty tedious.

She shook her head and opened her journal, then reread her last entry.

I really feel confused about tonight. I know we had to report the break-in, but I can't stop thinking about Jennifer Mitchell. I feel like we betrayed her, even though she would have gotten in a lot of trouble with Rick Andover. I don't think John is completely objective about it either. He just wanted to keep her from running away, but I don't think he realizes how upset she's going to be. If Rick is arrested, she loses her boyfriend and her big plans all at the same time. I hope John realizes this whole thing isn't over yet.

Elizabeth chewed on the end of her pen, deep in thought. If Luke Lander had called the police the way he said he would, then Jennifer Mitchell was in for the shock of her life.

* * *

Jennifer flicked on the overhead light and checked her watch again: ten after twelve. Biting her lip, she shut the light off and shifted uncomfortably on the front seat of her mother's car. She drew a deep, shaky breath and then another to steady her frazzled nerves.

"Rick, where are you?" she whispered. Her voice was edged with panic. There had to be a reason why he was forty minutes late. There had to be. Or maybe she was early, she thought frantically. Maybe she had misunderstood his directions. For the hundredth time she went over their telephone conversation in her head.

"Are you all ready?" Rick had said when she answered the phone earlier in the evening.

"Yes—I've got everything I need," Jennifer assured him. Her heart was hammering with excitement and eagerness. Tonight would be the start of a whole new life. "I'm all packed and everything."

"Great. That's really good. Now, here's what we're going to do. I want you to meet me at the corner of Madison and LaBrea."

"OK. I'll leave a note for my mother to say where I left her car."

"Great. I've got some things to do first, some people to see, OK? So meet me at eleven-thirty sharp. Have you got that?"

Jennifer could hardly contain her elation. "Yes. Eleven-thirty, corner of Madison and LaBrea. Rick, this is so great. I know we'll make it."

"Sure we will, Jen. I gotta go, so I'll see you later, right?"

"Eleven-thirty. I'll be there." She squeezed her eyes shut as she added, "I love you."

Rick hung up before he heard her last sentence, but she didn't care. There would be plenty of time ahead to tell him how she felt about him.

She looked around her room triumphantly, glad it was the last time she would be in it for a long time, maybe even forever. When she came back to Sweet Valley, she would be a star. And everyone—especially her father—would have to eat their words about Rick. So all she had to do was wait until eleven-thirty, and her new life would start. . . .

But now it was past midnight, and there was no doubt in Jennifer's mind she had gotten the time right. She was in the right place at the right time, but Rick wasn't. In an agony of worry she looked through the back window again, checking the dark, empty streets for any sign of him. In the backseat her suitcase and her keyboard were a painful reminder of the cross-country trip that was supposed to have started that evening.

"What happened?" she pleaded in the darkness. "Where are you?"

Her heart lurched as a police car drove past her down the street. Quickly slumping down behind the steering wheel, she watched the police car disappear from view. For a few more minutes she resisted the urge to check the time again, but finally she couldn't stand it anymore. With trembling fingers she switched on the light and looked at her watch. She felt numb with worry and disbelief. Rick was over an hour late.

For the first time she began to wonder what would happen if he didn't show up at all. She couldn't sit in the car at an intersection all night, especially if the squad car passed her again and began to get suspicious. And if she and Rick had to leave on a different night, Jennifer didn't want to risk alerting her parents to the plan by staying out until dawn. If she lost the advantage of getting away secretly, she would never be able to leave.

"Rick, what should I do?" Jennifer could feel the chill night air seeping into the car. She shivered and hugged herself while she debated all the options. Sitting alone, waiting, not knowing—it was becoming a nightmare. She didn't know what to do, what to think.

At two o'clock in the morning she started the car and slowly drove home.

Six

Jennifer woke up with a jolt and lay staring at the ceiling while she tried to figure out what was wrong. Something terrible had happened, but her groggy mind couldn't grasp what it was. Then she remembered.

Rick.

With a muffled groan, she rolled over onto her side and pulled the pillow down over her head. Maybe it would all turn out to be a bad dream. Maybe—

"Jen? You up yet? I'm making pancakes!" Her mother's voice drifted into her room.

Jennifer pushed herself up and stared bleakly around her bedroom. "I shouldn't have left," she whispered. "He could have come after I left and thought I never showed up."

"Jen?"

"I'm coming!" she managed to call back. She

got up and checked to make sure she had completely pushed her suitcase under her bed the night before. If there was any chance the plan would still go through, she didn't want to blow it by letting her parents see her packed luggage or the note about the car, which she had ripped to shreds.

"I thought you were going to sleep all day," Mrs. Mitchell said as Jennifer plodded into the kitchen. She turned from the stove with a wry look. "You were out awfully late last night."

"Mmm." Too worried and tired and depressed to bother with conversation, Jennifer slumped at the table and let out a heavy sigh. Across the room, her father was talking on the telephone.

"No kidding, Jack? Can't say I'm surprised, though." Mr. Mitchell looked over at Jennifer. Jack was Jack Parker, Jennifer knew, a lawyer at the district attorney's office and a friend of her father's. They frequently played tennis together on weekends.

"Have some juice, honey? Fresh-squeezed." Mrs. Mitchell held up a glass invitingly.

Jennifer gave her mother a blank stare. She couldn't believe the world was still droning along so obliviously. It didn't feel right. "What?"

"I said do you want some juice? Really, Jen. I don't think you should stay out so late if you're going to be this tired," her mother said.

For a moment all Jennifer could do was stare

at her mother. It seemed impossible that her parents still treated her like a child, especially when she had almost run away from home the night before. She still loved her parents, but she knew things would never be the same between her and them. She drew a deep breath, then said, "I don't want anything, Mom. I'm not hungry."

"You have to have something, dear," Mrs. Mitchell insisted. "Come on, how about some pan—"

"I don't want any!" Covering her eyes with her hand, Jennifer slumped further in her chair and tried to concentrate. There had to be a reason why Rick hadn't shown up—and a reason why he hadn't tried getting in touch with her. At the moment she didn't feel like noticing the hurt look she knew would be on her mother's face, or apologizing. She just wanted— needed—to know what had happened.

"I don't want anything," she repeated in a tightly controlled voice. "I'm not hungry. I'll eat later."

"OK, Jack. Meet you at the courts at three. Bye." Mr. Mitchell hung up the phone and sat down across from Jennifer.

"That was Jack Parker, Jen," he announced, picking up his coffee cup. "He had some interesting news."

Jennifer didn't look up. She didn't care what Jack Parker had told her father.

"Jen?" Her father paused. "Your friend Rick Andover was arrested last night for burglary."

At the sound of Rick's name, Jennifer became rigid. And the news caused her mind to go blank for a moment. It couldn't be true.

"He broke into a music store and stole a very expensive guitar and some cash," Mr. Mitchell continued. His voice was sad, and his gaze rested on her pityingly.

Mrs. Mitchell exclaimed, "Oh, no! I knew he was a troublemaker, but this!" Turning to Jennifer, she added, "That's it for you, young lady. You're not seeing that boy ever again."

Jennifer's mind was a whirl of conflicting thoughts and emotions. On the one hand she felt a crazy sense of relief that Rick hadn't deliberately stood her up. But the next moment she was screaming at herself for being so selfish. The boy she loved had been arrested for burglary, and all she knew was that it had to be some kind of stupid mistake. *Rick might have his problems*, she told herself, *but he would never break into a store*.

"Jen? I said I don't want you to see that boy any more, do you understand?" Her mother broke into Jennifer's anguished reverie. "He's a criminal!"

"No, he's not!" Jennifer found her voice suddenly and shook her head. "He would never do that," she insisted, pushing her chair back abruptly. "It's a mistake."

Mr. Mitchell cleared his throat and gave her a warning glance. "It's no mistake, Jennifer. I told you he was heading for trouble, and now he's in it up to his neck."

"No!" Wide-eyed with indignation, Jennifer glared at her father. "I know he wouldn't. Someone set him up. He must have been framed!"

"Oh, come on, Jen! Be sensible!" Mr. Mitchell scoffed. "Who would bother to do that?" Shaking his head, he stood up and stalked to the stove to pour himself some more coffee. With his back to her, he added, "Nobody needed to frame Rick Andover, he did it all by himself."

Something in her father's tone made Jennifer suspicious. She was convinced someone had framed Rick, and a glimmer of an idea had just occurred to her. If her father had eavesdropped on her phone call with Rick the night before—if he knew they were planning to run away together—he could have set Rick up in order to throw a wrench into their plans. Mr. Mitchell had never made a secret of how much he despised Rick. Putting him in jail was just the sort of thing her father would do, Jennifer decided with growing certainty.

As the idea took shape in her mind, Jennifer thought she remembered the faint click of another phone extension being replaced before she had hung up the phone. In an instant she was absolutely sure that her father *had* listened in. It was all her father's fault that Rick had been arrested. A feeling of cold, bitter anger filled Jennifer as she watched her father sit down again across from her and pick up the newspaper.

"You ruined my life," she said in a low, intense voice. She stood up unsteadily and grabbed the edge of the table. She had never been so furious and upset in her life. The cruelty and unfairness of what her father had done almost blinded her for a moment. Her mind was reeling.

Mr. Mitchell lowered the paper, a look of bafflement on his face. "What?"

"You know what I mean," Jennifer said. Her voice tightened in her throat as she continued. "I'll *never* forget this. I hate you! I *hate* you!" Bursting into tears, she turned and raced out of the kitchen.

Elizabeth sat up on her blanket and looked around. As usual for a Saturday afternoon, the Sweet Valley beach was mobbed. It made her smile to see so many familiar faces. Almost the entire student population of Sweet Valley High was there, lying on the sand or frolicking in the water.

"What are you grinning about?" Jeffrey asked.

She turned to him with arched eyebrows. "Was I smiling? I was just thinking—nothing in particular."

Jeffrey scooped up a handful of sand and trickled it through his fingers onto her toes. "OK, be secretive and mysterious," he said in a lofty tone.

"That's my sister's department," Elizabeth returned. Their eyes met, and Elizabeth grinned. Then she rolled over onto her stomach to survey the beach again. Her twin was sitting with A.J. and Lila just a few feet away, and a group of juniors and seniors were playing volleyball. As Elizabeth squinted against the glare, she caught sight of Amy Sutton hurrying across the sand toward Jessica.

"You'll never believe what I heard!" Amy called out in a voice shrill with excitement. Some of the volleyball players called it quits and walked over as Amy arrived.

She knelt on Jessica's blanket and announced loudly, "Rick Andover was arrested for burglary last night! Isn't that unbelievable?"

"You're kidding!" Jessica exclaimed and scrambled onto her knees. "How do you know?"

"Yeah," Lila seconded, "how do you know?"

A small group of curious students had gathered around, waiting avidly for the rest of Amy's news bulletin. Elizabeth, lying with Jeffrey, followed the conversation without watching. A faint blush colored her cheeks as she listened, and when she saw John Pfeifer on the fringes of the crowd, she saw that he was looking self-conscious, too.

"My mom heard it in the newsroom," Amy explained with an air of importance. Mrs. Sutton worked at a nearby television station, a fact that Amy managed to work into a lot of conversations. "He ripped off the Mello Music Shop downtown for a Fender Stratocaster guitar and a whole lot of money."

"He's the guy you were telling me about, right?" A.J. said to Jessica. She nodded, and he turned back to Amy. "Did they catch him doing it?"

Amy shook her head. "No—the police received an anonymous tip."

"Anonymous tip!" Lila repeated. She looked delighted.

Against her will, Elizabeth met John's eyes again. She felt somewhat uncomfortable about her role in Rick Andover's arrest, even though she knew she had done the right thing. But she hadn't told anyone about it, not even Jeffrey. John looked away.

"I'm not surprised." Bruce Patman picked up his Frisbee and bounced it on the heel of his hand. As a senior, a varsity tennis team star, and a member of one the richest families in Sweet Valley, Bruce had an ego the size of California. "I always said that guy would end up on a chain gang. Now it looks like he's on his way," he drawled. He tossed back his thick black hair and smiled scornfully.

An excited buzz of conversation started up, and everyone began speculating about the burglary and arrest. Old stories about Rick Andover's recklessness were tossed out again, and new ones circulated at the same time.

Elizabeth stood up suddenly. She didn't want to hear any more. Deep in thought, she wandered off down the beach, kicking the sand.

"Hi," came a voice from behind her.

She looked up suddenly but relaxed when she saw it was John. "Hi. I guess Mr. Lander did call the police. He said he would."

"Yeah. I guess so." John shrugged. "So the trip's off," he added with a sigh of relief.

Nodding, Elizabeth walked on a few more steps. Then she stopped and looked back at him. "Have you talked to her—Jennifer? She must be pretty upset."

"Well . . ." John hesitated for a moment. Then, with a sheepish look, he admitted, "I called her house this morning, but Mrs. Mitchell said Jennifer wouldn't come to the phone for anyone."

Elizabeth nodded, not meeting his eyes. "Oh—I guess you can understand how she feels."

"Right."

"It's all for the best," Elizabeth went on hurriedly. She looked at John again, meeting his gaze evenly. "It would have been a disaster. . . ."

He nodded. "Right. A disaster." With a matter-of-fact smile, he added, "Well, thanks for help-ing out and everything, Liz. See you later."

"Sure." Elizabeth returned his smile absently and watched him stride down to the water's edge. She knew they had done the right thing, but she still felt uncomfortable.

It's all over with, she told herself sternly. *And now it's up to John to straighten things out with Jennifer if he wants to.*

She strolled back to Jeffrey and the others.

"The perfect vacation is going somewhere like L.A. or New York City to go shopping, and then partying till dawn," Jessica was saying. "I mean, what's the point of a vacation if you can't get away from your same old boring routine?"

Elizabeth turned to Jeffrey, an amused look in her blue-green eyes. Shopping and partying *was* the same old routine for Jessica. Jeffrey just smiled slightly and shrugged. When Jessica presented her opinions, it was usually best to stay out of the conversation.

But it was obvious A.J. wasn't about to keep quiet. As he swept his thick red hair out of his eyes, he said, "Yeah, but with your kind of vacation, you get totally wiped out and you need another vacation just to rest." He grinned. "The best vacation would be something like going up to the mountains—doing a little climbing, a lit-tle fishing, reading some good books . . ."

"Oh, come on, A.J." Jessica groaned. She scrambled onto her knees and shook a fist in his face. "You never want to do anything really fun."

He laughed. "OK. We'll see. Who here would rather spend a vacation shopping and partying and who would rather go up to the mountains?" He appealed to Elizabeth and Jeffrey. "Jeffrey? Bloomingdale's or the Sierras?"

"The Sierras, definitely," Jeffrey replied instantly. "If Liz goes, too."

Jessica sent Elizabeth a threatening look. Even though the argument was obviously for fun, Elizabeth could still recognize the determination in her twin's face. Jessica hated to be contradicted.

"Liz?" Jessica said. "Would you rather go to fabulous, exciting New York City or go break your leg and get mosquito bites in the mountains?"

"Hmm . . ." Grinning, Elizabeth looked from Jessica to A.J. and back again. "I don't think I want to get roped into this," she said. Her eyes danced with amusement as Jessica pretended to strangle A.J. "Are you trying to eliminate the competition?" Elizabeth asked lightly.

Jessica looked over at her, an innocent expression on her face. "That's right." She went back to strangling A.J., and he made mock choking noises.

"OK, Jess. I agree with you," Elizabeth spoke up.

Jessica let go of A.J.'s neck and smiled. "Thank you."

"I change my vote, too," Jeffrey said. Looking at A.J., he explained, "Only because I don't want to see you murdered."

A.J. flopped backward onto the sand and let out a gasp. "I give up. I'd rather shop."

"That's what I thought you meant," Jessica said. She sent Elizabeth a triumphant look before lounging on the sand beside her boyfriend.

Elizabeth shook her head, still smiling. But inwardly she was disturbed. To everyone else it seemed like just a silly, unimportant argument. But Elizabeth knew Jessica was earnest. And she wondered how much longer Jessica and A.J. could go on disagreeing so strongly without having it affect their romance.

Seven

"Don't forget, I'll be collecting your dissection reports at the end of class," Mr. Hamilton announced. The biology teacher made his way around the different stations, commenting on the dissections in progress. Jennifer watched him distractedly. Finally he reached her side.

"How's it coming?" he asked, giving her an encouraging smile.

Jennifer blushed, and shrugged noncommittally. She was going through the motions without caring about the project at all. "I—OK, I guess."

"Any questions?"

How about "Would you please leave me alone?" she asked him silently. She didn't want to be there and didn't care what kind of digestive system an earthworm had. It all seemed so pointless that she could have screamed.

And the way people had been looking at her since Monday—she didn't care about that, either. It was Wednesday, and she had been living this nightmare for five days, but she couldn't help noticing the speculative glances, the undisguised curiosity in the other students' faces. Everyone knew by now she had been going out with Rick and that he was in jail. Any scrap of scandal would make their day, she thought bitterly. But she wasn't going to give them the satisfaction of seeing her get upset.

They can all jump in the ocean, she said to herself. *I never want to talk to any of them again.*

None of them could understand how *she* felt as a result of Rick's arrest. No one could know how hurt and betrayed she felt. Her heart was like a tight knot inside her chest. Knowing that her father, who had always been so fair and dependable, could have stabbed her in the back this way . . .

Jennifer squeezed her eyes shut to blot out her thoughts, but the pain didn't go away. For the rest of the class, she thought about how much she missed Rick. Then she handed in her report and escaped into the hallway. Just going through the motions of her life hurt so much, she was almost numb.

"Hi. Wait up."

The familiar voice stopped Jennifer as she

hurried to the stairs. At least there was one person she could bear talking to. She turned to face John Pfeifer.

"Hi," she echoed.

He shifted his books from one hand to the other. "What's your next class? English, right?"

"Right."

"Come on. I'm going that way, too." Without a backward glance, John set off down the stairway.

Jennifer stared at his back for a moment, slightly surprised. In five days John hadn't asked a single question about Rick's arrest, hadn't said anything about her botched plans to go to New York. Nothing. He was just the same old friendly, dependable John.

Halfway down the stairs he stopped and turned around, giving her a questioning glance. "Coming?"

Nodding, she hugged her books to her chest and headed down. As she reached the step he was on, he matched his steps with hers, not speaking, as they continued together. Suddenly Jennifer felt a flicker of gratitude toward John. He was always so easy to get along with, so nonjudgmental. There wasn't even a hint of curiosity in him, even though he knew better than anyone how much she loved Rick and what a disaster his arrest was for her. And she knew if she ever felt like talking about it, John would be there to listen, just as he'd always been.

But I can't talk about it yet—it hurts too much.

"Well, see you later," John said.

Startled, she looked up. They were outside her English class, and John was smiling at her with his usual warm, open smile. For some reason that smile hurt her. Her throat tight, she nodded and turned to go inside.

"Hi, Jennifer," Lila Fowler said with a fake smile. She was just leaving the room for her own next class, and her light brown eyes glittered with malicious curiosity. "Did you find out yet who put Rick in jail?"

Jennifer darted a pained look at Lila and hurried to her seat without answering. She already knew who had put Rick in jail. It was her own father. And that was why it hurt so much.

"Now, come on," Jessica said in a coaxing tone. She dragged A.J. toward the Sweet Valley High tennis courts and grinned at him impishly. "A basketball star like you—you can play tennis. It's simple. A nice, relaxing after-school game."

A.J. dragged his feet, but he smiled back at her, his eyes dancing with laughter. "Sure, Jess. Sure."

"And besides," she went on in a challenging tone, "you can beat a *girl*, can't you?"

"Depends on the girl," A.J. joked. He yelped as Jessica poked him in the ribs with her racket. Then he followed her in through the gate.

Jessica took a firm stance at the baseline at the opposite end of the court and bounced a ball a few times. "Now, most important is follow-through, A.J." She looked at him over the net. He looked fantastic in tennis whites, she thought. She decided it was the way his white shirt emphasized his red hair and his tan that made him so irresistible. A.J. was a natural athlete, and she knew he could play tennis if he tried. And since she played tennis a lot, she wanted him to try.

Grinning, Jessica blew A.J. a kiss, then sent him an ace serve. He swiped wildly with his racket and stumbled backward.

"Hey! Wakefield, you watch it," he said, scowling severely.

"Oops. Sorry." She gave him another innocent, angelic smile and paused for a moment to watch a slim, auburn-haired girl walk onto the next court with a hopper of balls. While Jessica watched, the girl plucked two balls from the basket, pocketed one and tossed the other up into the air. In a blinding flash she brought up her racket and sent the ball smashing across the net.

"Nice serve!" Jessica called out. She gave the girl an appraising look. She had seen her around school a few times but wasn't sure what her name was.

"I'm Jessica Wakefield, and this is A.J. Morgan." A.J. saluted with his racket.

"Hi, I'm Kristin Thompson."

Jessica recognized the name of Sweet Valley's up-and-coming tennis star. "Maybe we can hit a few balls sometime."

To her surprise Jessica noticed that Kristin was trying not to smile. "Well—OK. Sometime," the girl said in a neutral tone.

Jessica nodded haughtily, annoyed. She didn't need anyone patronizing *her*. Turning back to A.J., she put Kristin Thompson out of her mind. She was there to concentrate on her boyfriend, after all. "OK. Watch out, Morgan—and keep your racket back!"

Jennifer sat in stony silence at the dinner table on Wednesday night, picking at her food. When she first realized what her father had done, she refused to eat with her parents at the table. But her mother insisted. "Eat with us like a civilized person, or don't eat at all," she said.

But that didn't mean she had to look at her

father, talk to him, or acknowledge his existence. It had been five days now, and Jennifer hadn't relented one bit.

"How's school?" Mr. Mitchell said in a tight voice.

Jennifer deliberately picked up her glass of milk and began drinking it, her eyes straight ahead. A tense, uncomfortable silence echoed through the room.

"Jennifer Holland Mitchell—"

"Honey!" Mrs. Mitchell interrupted hastily, shaking her head. "She'll come around," she continued in an irritated tone.

"I will not come around." Jennifer spoke to her mother coldly. She glared at Mrs. Mitchell for a moment, aggravated because her mother wasn't bothering to return the look. Unexpectedly, though, her mother's face underwent a change as Jennifer watched. A look of alarm passed across it.

"Brian—are you all right?"

Mr. Mitchell dropped his knife and fork on the plate and let out a stifled grunt of pain. "Just heartburn," he muttered.

Good. Now you know how I feel, Jennifer raged at him silently. *My heart feels like it's been burned to a crisp.*

"It's this case—it's driving me up a wall," he went on. Mr. Mitchell's current court case had

70

been dragging on for weeks, constantly getting bogged down in technicalities.

"Well, why don't you go take some antacid and lie down," Mrs. Mitchell suggested. Turning to Jennifer, she added, "And I'd like you to clear the table and wash up. Then take out the trash." Her tone was severe.

Jennifer raised her gaze briefly to her mother's face. If her mother thought tough treatment would make her forgive her father, she was completely wrong.

I'll never forgive him for what he did, Jennifer vowed.

On Friday at lunch John went to the newspaper office to finish up a story about the girls' basketball team. The cluttered *Oracle* staff room was empty and quiet, and he sat for a while, musing. He couldn't help remembering the conversation he had had there with Elizabeth, when he had asked her for advice about Jennifer.

Elizabeth had been right as usual, John thought. He was confident that Jennifer would get over losing Rick before long. At least she was still in Sweet Valley and not in New York. That was something to be glad about, and Jennifer still thought of him as a friend. As for

71

Rick Andover, he was still in custody, awaiting a hearing.

John was staring absently at the door when it opened and Jennifer stepped inside. He gaped at her, almost believing for a second that he was imagining her, since he had just been thinking about her. But she really was there.

"Hi," she said shyly. She twisted a strand of her long blond hair and looked around the office. Her brown eyes turned back to him after a moment. "I had a feeling you'd be here."

"Hi." Coming to his senses, John stood up from his chair and took a step toward her. He couldn't believe she had come looking for him! A warm flood of happiness washed over him. It actually could be the start of a whole new relationship for them!

"Well, you were right," he added, feeling stupid. His cheeks grew pink as he looked at her. "I'm just working on a story."

She rewarded him with a soft, wistful smile. "I won't bother you if you're busy. I can come back some other time."

"No—come on, sit down. I'm finished. Actually, I'm not really doing anything."

He watched in hopeful silence as she sank into a chair and propped her elbows up on the big conference table. She looked so forlorn and sad, he was tempted to go right over and hug her. "Everything OK?" he asked, fighting the urge.

"I don't know," she said after a moment's thought. "I feel so—lost. Like I don't know what to do."

John nodded in sympathy. "I know. It's really rotten luck."

"Luck?" she scoffed. Her tone was surprisingly hard. "If you call having a mean, devious father who'd rather ruin your life than give you a shot at happiness bad luck . . ." Her voice trailed off, and she jutted her chin out stubbornly.

A feeling of uneasiness settled in John's stomach. He grabbed the nearest chair and sat down quickly. He swallowed. "What do you mean about your father?"

Jennifer drew a deep breath. "You know what he did? This is all his fault! That night when Rick and I were going to leave, my father listened to us on the phone, and then he called the police to frame Rick! That's what I mean," she concluded, her voice heavy with scorn and anger.

"How—do you know?"

"Oh, come on! It's obvious, isn't it? Besides, who else would have done it?" Jennifer said vehemently. "He did it—and I hate him for it. I hate him so much I could scream."

Stunned, John sat staring at Jennifer, trying to absorb her harsh, bitter words.

This wasn't supposed to happen! he cried silently. *This is all wrong!*

From knowing the Mitchell family for so long, John knew Jennifer really loved her father. So for her to hate him now showed how upset and disappointed she was about Rick. And for her to ignore the evidence—Rick *did* have the stolen guitar when he was arrested, after all—meant she was too distraught to listen to reason. He knew he couldn't let her go on blaming her father for something he didn't do.

But if I tell her I called the police, she'll hate me instead, John thought.

"You never really know someone, do you?" Jennifer was saying. She slumped in her chair. "It's so hard to know who you can really trust."

John nodded, too confused and frustrated to say anything. He felt like the biggest liar in the world, but he couldn't stand the thought of telling Jennifer the truth. He sensed she was opening up to him in a new way and that it might lead to something else—something wonderful. He couldn't risk losing that. Not now, not when he was so close.

"I know what you mean," he heard himself saying.

"Except you." Jennifer gave him a long, measuring look. Her large brown eyes were thoughtful as she said, "I always knew I could trust you. It's like we've known each other for so long—I don't know." She looked away. "I'm not making any sense."

Through clenched teeth he repeated, "I know what you mean."

There was a short silence. Jennifer stared across the newspaper office, seemingly far away, and John sat, feeling miserable, watching her.

I have to say something—it's not fair, one side of his conscience argued.

But I can tell she's starting to think differently about me—I can tell, the other side insisted.

"Well," she began, pushing her chair back, "I should probably—"

At that moment the public-address speaker hummed, and there was a crackling sound as someone blew into the microphone. "Attention," came one of the secretary's voices. "Attention, please. Will Jennifer Mitchell please come to the administration office immediately. Jennifer Mitchell to the administration office."

Jennifer was frozen. She stared at the speaker up on the wall with wide, terrified eyes. Slowly she turned to look at John. "It's Rick—something's happened to him!"

John's stomach tightened at the anxious note in her voice. She was still in love with Rick.

I should've known, he told himself. *You're a jerk to think she could start to like you already.*

75

"You'd better go and find out," he said. He hoped his voice didn't betray how hurt he felt.

"Come with me, please?" Jennifer said, pleading with her eyes.

John pushed himself up from his chair. "Sure. No problem. Let's go."

In silence they hurried through the building to the administration office. John stole a quick glance at Jennifer as they walked and wasn't surprised to see an expression of fearful concern on her face.

"Hi, I'm Jennifer Mitchell," she said as they entered the office.

The secretary looked up and nodded tersely. Her expression was grave. "Your mother just phoned from the hospital, Jennifer. Your father is sick. I'll give you a pass to excuse you from the rest of school."

John felt as if he had been punched in the stomach. Without thinking, he reached for Jennifer's hand. "Come on," he said, pulling her out into the hall again. "I'll take you to the hospital."

"No." She yanked her hand away and planted herself firmly where she stood. "I don't want to go."

He stared at her. "But, Jen—your father—"

"No! I don't have anything to say to him," she insisted coldly.

Sick with guilt, John stood staring at her, not knowing what to say. It was *his* fault that she felt this way about her father. If it weren't for him, she would rush to the hospital to be with her father.

"Jennifer—I—"

"Please back me up on this, John." Jennifer looked up at him with a hurt, tearful expression in her eyes. "You're the only friend I have now."

Against his will, John felt himself nod. He couldn't say no when she put it that way. "All right," he said hoarsely. "Whatever you say."

Eight

Jessica flopped into a chair across from Amy Sutton and snapped open a can of soda. "Mondays are such a bore." She groaned. The weekend had gone by like a flash, over before it even started, it seemed. "The whole week to get through—sometimes I feel like I spend my whole life at school."

Next to her at the cafeteria table Lila picked fastidiously at a plate of chicken salad. "Tell me about it," she muttered.

"Maybe all we need is a little excitement," Amy suggested. She threw a speculative look around the crowded cafeteria. "Something to stir things up."

"How about some new guys?" Lila cocked one eyebrow and shrugged. "That would be a major improvement."

Jessica snorted. Lila had already dated most

of the decent available boys at school. In fact, she seemed to go through dates as quickly as arrogant Bruce Patman did.

"Maybe some new categories in the slam books," Amy mused. "Some really juicy ones."

The slam books had been Amy's most recent contribution to Sweet Valley High social life. Marbled notebooks with each page headed "Most Flirtatious" or "Biggest Jock" or some other category were circulated around the school. Anonymously, everyone filled in a name under each category, and the results had really caused a sensation.

"How about 'Most Likely to End Up in Jail for Tax Evasion'?" Jessica offered with a grin. "I bet Lila gets a lot of votes."

"Lila's accountant, you mean," Amy corrected her.

Lila gave them both a withering look. "Please. Spare me." Lila's father was one of the richest men in Sweet Valley, and Lila often complained about her trust funds and tax shelters.

A mischievous gleam came into Lila's eyes, though. She put down her fork carefully and twined her fingers together. "Actually, there are some things we should find out—off the record."

Amy sat up straighter, looking interested. "What do you mean?"

"Well—like 'Best Kisser,' " Lila explained. "I

know for a fact that every girl automatically put in her own boyfriend, but that doesn't necessarily follow, you know. It's not impartial."

Jessica let out a giggle. "Maybe we should do some field research—"

"Take a survey," Amy cut in, laughing. "Serious hands-on research."

Lila hooted. "Or we could interview Jess. She's dated half the boys in school—"

"And you've dated the other half," Jessica interrupted. She tapped her cheek thoughtfully. "I hate to admit it, but Bruce is pretty good, believe me."

Amy smirked. "I know."

"But so is Tom McKay—"

"Out of bounds," Lila interrupted with a giggle. "He's taken."

Rolling her eyes, Amy huffed, "Well, practically everyone's going out with someone."

Jessica hitched her chair closer, her blue-green eyes dancing. As she started to speak she noticed A.J. walking toward her. In a conspiratorial tone she said, "Well, when my cousin Kelly went out with Kirk Anderson—"

"Kirk the Jerk," Amy supplied. She grimaced in anticipation. "Yeah? Yeah?"

"According to her, he's definitely in the major leagues."

"You mean according to *him*," Lila insisted.

The girls erupted into shrieks of laughter as A.J. pulled out a chair next to Jessica.

"Hi. What's so funny?" he asked, smiling.

Jessica caught her breath. "We were just trying to figure out—"

"Officially," Lila said, giggling.

Amy waved her hand. "Officially *off* the record."

Jessica silenced her friends with a firm look. "We were trying to figure out who's really the best kisser at Sweet Valley High."

A.J. looked at her blankly, and his smile faded. "Oh."

Instantly Jessica regretted having told him. From the first, A.J. had let her know that he didn't like really flirtatious, boy-crazy girls. Originally he'd had the impression that Jessica was the quiet, shy type and that was why he had been attracted to her. Since then he had gotten used to her outgoing behavior, but still . . .

"It's not like you're the first guy I ever dated," Jessica reminded him. A.J. didn't say anything, and Jessica began to wish she had kept quiet. She scooted her chair close and gave him a seductive look. "Actually," she began again, trying to mollify him, "I think *you're* the best kisser at school."

A.J. flushed scarlet. "Thanks for the recommendation," he said in a tight, sarcastic voice. He abruptly pushed his chair back and stood up. "Listen, I have to go. I'll see you later."

An awkward silence fell as A.J. stalked away. Jessica let out a sigh of frustration.

"What's with him?" Lila drawled, breaking the tension.

Jessica replied in a petulant tone, "I don't know. He gets embarrassed over the dumbest things sometimes. You'd think he'd be flattered."

"He didn't look very flattered to me," Amy observed. She eyed Jessica curiously. "You two having trouble?"

"No!" Jessica snapped. She restrained another angry retort and picked up her soda. "No trouble at all."

After school on Tuesday, John met Jennifer in the parking lot. At lunch he had hesitantly invited her up to Secca Lake, and to his amazement she agreed. He still couldn't get over the way she was leaning on him, looking to him for support and friendship.

And maybe more, he added with a silent prayer. John knew he was head over heels in love with her. It was scary, but exciting at the same time.

Smiling shyly, he opened the car door for her and helped her get in. He felt very protective of her. In minutes they were headed up to the big park. As he drove, John kept stealing glances at Jennifer. He almost couldn't believe she was really there with him. It was too good to be true. More and more now, Jennifer actually came looking for *him*—to talk or just to spend some quiet moments alone together. She had said she felt comfortable and secure with him.

And the other thing he was secretly pleased about was that Rick's name was coming up less and less. Jennifer talked more about her father now than about Rick. Unfortunately, though, John couldn't make up his mind which was worse: that Jennifer blamed her father for betraying her, or that Jennifer might still be in love with Rick.

"Thanks for being so nice," Jennifer said softly. They were just pulling into the parking lot at Secca Lake. Ahead, the water stretched out calm and blue. Looking at her hands, she added, "You're the nicest guy I've ever known. You really understand me." She turned to him and gave him a warm, grateful smile.

John stared at her, speechless. More than anything else he wanted to kiss her. But he was afraid of pushing things. And he also felt a terrible burden of guilt whenever she looked at him that way. Mr. Mitchell was still in the hospital with a heart problem, and Jennifer hadn't even called him once.

"Don't you think—" he began hoarsely. "I mean, are you going to go see your father?"

The familiar stubborn look came into Jennifer's eyes again. "No. Stop asking me! I don't have anything to say to him. OK, so he's in the hospital, but my going there isn't going to change anything."

John thought she was wrong. He suspected that Mr. Mitchell would have a lot more hope and strength if he wasn't worrying about Jennifer. But John didn't want to aggravate her any further.

"Let's just not talk about him, please?" Jennifer asked. Wearily she leaned her head back against the seat and closed her eyes. "Someone who would do what he did to me—I just can't talk to him. Don't ask me to."

His throat tight, John nodded and looked away. He was in the worst mess he had ever been in in his life. Because of what he'd done, the girl he loved was starting to feel a whole new way about him. But if she ever found out what he'd done, she would hate him even more than she hated her father now.

When Elizabeth got home from school on Wednesday, she grabbed her recorder and a book of baroque flute solos and headed for the backyard. Prince Albert, the Wakefields' Labrador retriever, settled down beside her on the patio.

"You're not going to get a lot of sleep, Albert," Elizabeth said, chuckling. "I haven't practiced in a long time."

The dog thumped his tail.

Smiling, Elizabeth opened up her music and adjusted her recorder for tone. Then she ran through the first few measures of a piece she particularly liked. After a second or two of melody, she produced a shrill *sqeeeeep*!

"Yikes." Elizabeth made a sour face and frowned at her recorder. She had taken up playing it recently, and she really enjoyed it. Unfortunately, she hadn't *quite* perfected her technique.

Next to her, Prince Albert gave her a doubtful glance, then heaved himself up and padded slowly to the other side of the patio. Elizabeth laughed and turned back to her music. "I don't blame you, boy."

"Hello? Anyone home?" Elizabeth heard A.J. calling from around the side of the house.

She looked up in surprise. "I'm out on the patio," she called back.

In moments A.J. appeared. "Isn't Jessica home?" he asked.

"No," Elizabeth said. "Was she supposed to be?"

A.J. shrugged. "Well, I said I'd pick her up at three."

"She'll probably be home any second," said Elizabeth. "You know how she is."

"Yeah." A.J.'s voice was thoughtful. Suddenly he turned and looked at her very intently. "Liz, can I ask you something?"

She raised her eyebrows a fraction. "Sure. Is something wrong?"

"I don't know. That's what—that's what I wanted to ask you," he stammered. Coloring slightly, he continued. "Do you think Jess is getting bored with me?"

For a moment Elizabeth just stared at him. Her twin was crazy about A.J. and had been ever since meeting him. But apparently something wasn't completely right between them. "I—I don't think so," she faltered. "No. She doesn't think you're at all boring."

A.J. nudged a fallen leaf with one toe. "I just thought— Never mind."

Just then a car door slammed out front. As they waited in silence, Elizabeth and A.J. heard pounding footsteps race through the house and up the stairs. Then all was quiet again. Elizabeth and A.J. exchanged a meaningful look.

"Jessica!" Elizabeth called out.

An upstairs window was flung open abruptly, and Jessica stuck her head out. "A.J.! Hi! You're here already! I'll be down in half a second." Then she disappeared just as suddenly.

Elizabeth turned to A.J. with a mixture of relief and exasperation. "See? I told you. She's just late, as usual."

"I guess you're right," he answered, grinning sheepishly. "Listen, you won't . . ." His voice trailed off.

Shaking her head, Elizabeth said, "I won't tell her what you asked, don't worry. See you later."

Waving, A.J. stood up and strolled into the house. A few moments later Elizabeth heard a series of distinctive noises: Jessica's feet thumping down the stairs, Jessica's muffled laugh, the front door slamming, and A.J.'s car pulling into the street.

Deep in thought, Elizabeth sat back and stared moodily at her sheet music. More and more it seemed obvious that Jessica and A.J. weren't the perfect match she had thought they were for a while, although she could feel there was an undeniable attraction between them. But lately it seemed to her that A.J. was more committed to the relationship than Jessica.

I just hope I'm wrong, she mused. Then she shrugged philosophically. There wasn't any sense brooding about something she had no control over. She raised her recorder to her mouth again and drew a deep breath.

Just then the telephone rang.

"Arrgh! I'm never going to learn this stupid piece," she growled, getting up out of her chair. She slid open the patio door and ran to the kitchen to pick up the phone.

"Hi, Liz? It's John. John Pfeifer."

"Hi, John. What's up?" Elizabeth leaned against the refrigerator.

"Well, I really need to talk to you about— about, you know. Jennifer and everything."

Elizabeth held back a sigh. "What's wrong?"

There was a pause. "Do you think you could meet me at school?" he asked. His voice sounded strained and worried. "I'm here now."

"Sure," Elizabeth replied.

So much for recorder practice, she told herself. But John was obviously very upset, and since they were both responsible for what had occurred, Elizabeth felt that she should go and meet him. "I'll come over now."

He sighed audibly. "Great. I'll be out at the playing fields."

Elizabeth checked her watch. "OK. I'll be there in about fifteen minutes."

"Good. And thanks, Liz."

When Elizabeth hung up the phone, she stood staring at it, wondering. She had thought everything was settled with John. After all, she had seen him and Jennifer together every day at school.

"There's something I don't understand, I guess," she said out loud. Shrugging, she picked up her car keys and walked out the front door.

Nine

Elizabeth hurried out toward the playing fields when she arrived at school. From a distance she could make out a solitary figure sitting high up in the bleachers. She lifted her hand in a wave as she reached the bottom step and started climbing.

"Hi, John."

"Liz, I can't believe this is happening," John began before she even sat down. His face was drawn and tense, his eyes wide with anxiety. He looked extremely upset.

Elizabeth took a seat quickly. "What? What's wrong?"

"It's Mr. Mitchell."

She nodded, looking serious and expectant.

"He's scheduled for heart bypass surgery to-morrow! Jennifer told me today at lunch!" John blurted out. He turned away, and his jaw muscles worked convulsively.

At first Elizabeth didn't know what to say. Of course she felt sympathetic, but she didn't understand why it was so urgent that John tell *her*. Trying not to sound too confused, she said, "That's too bad. But I don't see why—"

"Why I dragged you out here?" John finished for her. He rubbed both hands across his face and closed his eyes for a moment.

"John, what is it?" Elizabeth pressed. His expression was beginning to worry her. He looked both angry and ashamed. *"What?"*

John drew a shuddering breath. When he spoke, his voice was barely audible. "Jennifer thinks her father was the one who got Rick Andover arrested. She hasn't even spoken to him since that night, and she won't go to see him in the hospital."

Speechless, Elizabeth stared at him. Finally she managed to gasp, "Why? Didn't you ever tell her?"

"No," John groaned. He buried his face in his hands. A few moments later he looked up and met her shocked stare evenly. "I meant to, honest. And then she started really leaning on me, wanting to talk everything over—" He broke off and swallowed with difficulty.

Elizabeth nodded slowly. She could imagine Jennifer turning to John, looking for comfort.

And she could imagine how John had responded. It must have made him ecstatic.

"But then she started talking about how she figured out her father had listened in on the phone when she was talking with Rick and how he'd betrayed her," John went on. "She was talking about how much she hated him for what he did. I couldn't tell her it was really me!"

"Because then she'd hate you instead." Elizabeth looked out across the soccer field. In spite of the blazing sun, she felt a shiver go through her.

"You got it," he agreed in a bitter tone.

Elizabeth turned to him and looked searchingly into his eyes. "But, John, you have to tell her."

He returned her look silently.

"John!"

"I know. I know I do." Gritting his teeth, he added, "I can't let her hate him for something I did. Don't you think I know that?"

"Especially now that he's in the hospital," Elizabeth pointed out. She felt sad as she thought of Mr. Mitchell, sick and in pain, thinking that his daughter hated him.

And then she had a sobering thought: She was as responsible as John for turning Rick Andover in. The only reason she hadn't said anything to Jennifer was because she had assumed John had straightened everything out.

But now Elizabeth knew it would be as much her fault as John's if Jennifer went on accusing Mr. Mitchell wrongly.

"John, you have to tell her, or else I will," Elizabeth said in a hollow voice. "If anything happens to Mr. Mitchell during surgery—"

"It won't." John spoke harshly, his jaw set. Looking away, he insisted, "Nothing will happen."

"But what if it does?" Elizabeth grabbed his wrist and shook it. "John, what if he *dies*?"

John didn't say anything, but he seemed to be struggling for words. Finally he said, "If I tell her, she'll never speak to me again—especially now, since I kept it from her for so long."

Elizabeth's thoughts were in a whirl. John's news had taken her completely by surprise, but now, all of a sudden, she had a momentous decision to make. She knew that if Mr. Mitchell died thinking Jennifer hated him, she could never live with herself. Not when it was within her power to set the record straight.

She cast an anguished look at her friend. Deep down, she knew he was a decent, caring person. And she knew he would ultimately do the right thing. It was a question of timing, though. Even with good intentions, John might just keep putting off telling Jennifer, waiting for the right moment. Obviously he was afraid of jeopardizing the relationship he had wanted for so long. Now that it was in his grasp, he couldn't risk throwing it away.

But at the same time, she knew Jennifer had to be told, no matter what the consequences were. It was terribly wrong to keep the truth from her.

"I think you should tell her right now," Elizabeth said.

John turned to her, a bleak expression in his eyes. There was a long, expectant pause. Then he nodded. "I know," he said hoarsely. "I will."

Elizabeth let out a sigh of relief. "Do you have your car here? I can drive you over to her house," she added when he shook his head. She stood up and held out her hand. "Come on. Let's go right now."

He stared at her hand for a moment as though he weren't really seeing it. Then he looked up and gave her a painful, twisted smile. "OK. We might as well get it over with. Let's go."

John sat in silence all the way to the Mitchells' house. A strange feeling of unreality gripped him as they got closer and closer. *I can't believe I'm really going through with this*, he thought. *I can't believe I have to do this.*

There was a tight lump in his throat that he tried hard to swallow. He cast a brief look of distress at Elizabeth when they pulled up in front of the familiar house. There was no way to avoid it, he knew. As he shouldered open his door, Elizabeth said, "I'll wait for you."

All the way up the path he kept his eyes firmly locked on the front door. He was afraid he would suddenly lose all courage at the last moment. But he knew in his heart he had to tell Jennifer the truth. If he didn't, there was no way they could have a relationship. He would always know he was deceiving her.

So either way I lose. At least this way I'm being completely honest with her.

His heart pounding, John knocked on the door. He waited for what seemed like an hour before he heard footsteps in the hallway beyond.

"John! Hi." Jennifer greeted him with a puzzled smile. She had a can of soda in her hand. "What's up?"

"I have to talk to you," he said. He licked his lips and dug his hands into his pockets. Looking over her shoulder, he added, "Are you alone?"

She rolled her eyes. "Mom's at the hospital, as usual. Yeah, I'm alone."

Without trying to explain, he pushed past her and stalked into the living room. It was a familiar, comfortable room. He had been there dozens of times throughout his childhood. And he knew he might never be invited back after what he was about to say.

Jennifer followed him in and hitched herself up on the arm of a wing chair. "John? What's wrong? You look so pale."

"Listen. I have to tell you something." He whirled around to face her. "I'm the one who turned Rick in that night."

Jennifer stared at him blankly. "What? What are you talking about?"

"That night when Rick was arrested," he went on angrily. He could see it wasn't sinking in. Jennifer was so convinced her father had betrayed her that she couldn't comprehend what he was saying. She was just gaping at him in total confusion.

He scowled at her, furious with himself, with everything. "I was following him, and I saw him break into the music store. I called Luke Lander, and Luke Lander called the police. Your dad didn't have anything to do with it!"

As he watched, the color drained from Jennifer's face. Instantly she stood up and took a step backward, and a look of loathing came into her eyes. "You—*you?* You were *spying* on Rick?"

"Well, yeah! I didn't trust him, and it turns out I was right," John exploded.

Everything was going wrong. Instead of being sorry, he was acting as though he were mad at her. And in a way he *was* mad at her—for being so blind about Rick Andover when everyone else could see what a rat he was.

John sank onto the couch. "Look, I'm sorry," he said wearily, staring down at the floor. He couldn't look at Jennifer. "I know it was a lousy thing to do to you, but I didn't want to see you hurt for what he did. And I don't want you to blame your father for it."

"Dad." It came out in a whisper. Jennifer looked away and blinked. Her eyes were suddenly swimming with tears.

"Jen—" Instinctively, John stretched out his hands to her. He couldn't stand to see the pain in her face.

But she glared at him and stopped him dead. "You let me go on hating my father."

John nodded. "I know, but I—"

"I don't care what your excuse is," she cried, wiping away a tear. "All I know is I have to go to the hospital and tell him." She turned and strode out to the hallway and stopped.

John looked at her rigid back. It seemed to emanate pain and anger and disappointment. "Do you need a ride?" he asked nervously.

Jennifer glared fiercely at him but growled, "Yes. I do."

"Liz Wakefield drove me over," he explained as he walked closer to her. "I'm sure she'll give us a ride."

Without answering, Jennifer stalked outside ahead of him, heading for Elizabeth's red Fiat.

John caught Elizabeth's gaze and gave her a distraught look. Elizabeth saw and nodded.

"Can you give me a ride to the hospital, Elizabeth?" Jennifer asked. Her voice was tightly controlled but about to break.

"Sure. No problem. But you guys will have to double up. As you can see, there's a small backseat, but it's full of Jessica's stuff. She was supposed to clean it out, but if you know Jessica . . ."

A flush of embarrassment washed over John as he clambered into the passenger seat. Jennifer sat stiffly on his lap, as though she couldn't stand to touch him but didn't have a choice. It was hard for him to have her so close. He could feel how angry she was by her tense, unyielding muscles.

The three were absolutely silent as Elizabeth maneuvered the car through traffic. Across town, they entered the parking lot of Joshua Fowler Memorial Hospital and found a parking space near the main entrance.

Jennifer didn't say a word. She just jumped out and hurried to the door without looking back. In the car, Elizabeth and John exchanged a look.

"How did she take it?" Elizabeth asked softly.

John swallowed hard and shrugged. "How do you think?" he choked out, looking away. "Come on."

When they got to the main desk, they were just in time to see the elevator doors close. Jennifer was already on her way up.

"What room is Mr. Brian Mitchell in, please?" Elizabeth asked the receptionist.

After consulting a computer terminal, the woman said, "Five-thirty-eight. But you can't go up there. That's in ICU."

John grabbed Elizabeth's hand and pulled her to the elevators. "Come on."

"Did you hear what she said?" Elizabeth whispered as they dodged into an open elevator. John nodded grimly and pushed the button for the seventh floor. "He's in Intensive Care."

John didn't answer.

The car sped upward. John could hear his heart beating behind his ribs. He couldn't think. He didn't want to think. At last the elevator came to a stop, and the doors slid open. When John stepped out into the corridor, the first people he saw were Jennifer and Mrs. Mitchell.

Jennifer whirled around to confront him. "You couldn't have told me an hour ago, could you?" she said in a choked, bitter voice.

A cold panic swept over John. He couldn't say anything.

Elizabeth came forward, an anxious look in her eyes. "Hello, Mrs. Mitchell, I'm Elizabeth Wakefield. Is Mr. Mitchell all right?"

Jennifer's mother drew a deep breath. "He

took a turn for the worse this afternoon. They moved up the bypass surgery. He's being operated on now.''

The words sent a shock through John, and he turned to look helplessly at Jennifer. If her father didn't pull through, Jennifer would never have the chance to apologize. And it would be his fault.

Ten

As Elizabeth watched, Jennifer's face crumbled, and the girl burst into loud, uncontrollable sobs. Without warning, Jennifer punched John in the chest, and he staggered backward.

"Get out of here," she cried. "Just leave me alone."

Everyone stared at her, shocked.

"Jennifer! What are you doing?" Mrs. Mitchell said. She looked at John in embarrassed disbelief. "John, I'm sorry. I don't know why—"

"It's—it's my fault," he stammered, his face bright red. "I was the one—"

"Just get out of here," Jennifer repeated. She turned away and buried her face in her hands.

Her heart full, Elizabeth took John's arm firmly to steer him away. She gave Mrs. Mitchell an apologetic look. "I'm sorry. We'd better go. I hope Mr. Mitchell is all right." Turning to John, she added in an undertone, "Come on. It's a bad time, John."

"But I want to explain—" he began. Elizabeth shook her head.

The painful sound of Jennifer's crying filled the hushed hospital corridor. Reluctantly John let Elizabeth pull him away, and he looked at her with the most mournful expression she had ever seen.

"Come on," she repeated. She pulled him gently toward the elevator and led him inside. As the doors slid shut she let out a sigh. "I'm sorry, but I really thought it was better if we just left."

"You're right. But at least— I want to stay and wait," John corrected himself. He bit his lip and glanced at Elizabeth. "I want to make sure Mr. Mitchell's all right. Let's just wait downstairs."

Elizabeth thought it was a good idea to leave and let things settle down. There was nothing they could do for Mr. Mitchell, and Jennifer certainly didn't want any comfort from them. But Elizabeth could understand how John felt. She had waited in hospital waiting rooms before herself. When her best friend, Enid Rollins, had undergone back surgery, Elizabeth had waited for hours. Knowing she couldn't be any possible use to her friend hadn't deterred her then. And it wasn't deterring John now.

The elevator opened onto the main lobby, and John walked out, his hands deep in his pockets. Elizabeth suppressed a troubled sigh and followed him slowly into the lounge.

"He's got to pull through," John was saying under his breath. Scowling fiercely, he paced back and forth.

Elizabeth perched on the edge of a chair and watched him in silence. She wished there was something she could do to lighten his burden of guilt. Her heart ached to see how torn apart John was.

She glanced apprehensively at the wall clock, then crossed to the receptionist's desk. "Excuse me. I was wondering, is there any news about Mr. Mitchell's condition? He's in surgery right now," she explained.

The duty nurse gave her a sympathetic but regretful smile. "I'm sorry, I can only give out information on patients to members of the family."

"But—" Elizabeth cast an agonized look over at John. He was slumped in a chair. She turned back to the nurse. "We're friends of the family. We just wanted to know—"

"I'm sorry." The nurse shook her head firmly. "It's against hospital rules."

Elizabeth nodded in defeat and walked back to John. He raised his head and stared at her blankly as she approached. "They won't tell us anything, John. Even if we stay, we won't know how he is."

"Liz . . ." He squeezed his eyes shut. "I feel so helpless."

"Come on. Let me take you home. Even if it all turns out fine, Jennifer probably won't want to talk to you for a while."

"If ever," John added bitterly. But he nodded and looked her in the eyes. "You're right, though. There's no point in staying here."

"I know I'm right." Elizabeth breathed a sigh of relief and lightly touched his arm. "Come on."

John followed her silently, dragging his feet. In the car, though, he let out his anger. "I was only trying to help her, and I made such a giant mess!" he said. He pounded the car door with his fist. "What a loser."

Elizabeth turned in her seat and looked at him squarely. "Listen," she told him in a firm voice, "you're not a loser, John. You thought you were doing the right thing—you *did* do the right thing. And only because you care so much. That doesn't make you a loser."

"Yeah, sure, Liz."

She looked at him silently for another moment. She knew it would take some time for him to stop being so hard on himself. There wasn't anything more she could do, even though it broke her heart to see how much he was suffering. Without another word she started the Fiat and drove him home.

By the time Elizabeth got to her own house, she was sunk in gloom. She knew telling Luke Lander about Rick Andover's break-in had been the right thing to do. After all, she and John had witnessed a crime being committed. But since then, things had really gotten messed up. And it had all started with John asking her for some simple advice, too. When she thought back to how worried John had been at the beginning, she couldn't hold back a half-smile. If he had known then how much worse things were going to get, he probably would have been happy to have kept things the way they were.

Sighing, she pulled into the driveway and climbed slowly out of the Fiat. She stood for a moment, breathing in the warm, fragrant air. It had been a long time since she had felt so drained. Finally she walked to the back door and let herself into the kitchen, where Jessica was busy rinsing salad ingredients.

"Where have you been?" Jessica huffed. She brushed aside a stray wisp of hair with the back of one hand and gave Elizabeth a baleful look. "I thought you were going to help me get dinner ready. I already started the lasagna."

"Sorry."

Jessica arched her eyebrows. "So where've you been?"

"At the hospital. Jennifer Mitchell's father is having an operation," she said hastily as Jessica's eyes widened. "I drove her over with John Pfeifer."

Her twin just stared at her. "Since when do you drive around Jennifer Mitchell and John Pfeifer?" she demanded. She rolled her eyes in exasperation. "I swear, you let people just walk all over you. Anything they want, you do."

"That's not true, Jess, and you know it." Elizabeth leaned back against the counter and crossed her arms, brooding. She was in no mood to argue with her sister.

"Right," Jessica retorted sarcastically. She rinsed off a tomato and dried it vigorously, then darted a speculative look at her sister. "You're never going to *believe* what happened," she said, abruptly changing the subject.

Elizabeth pushed herself away from the counter. As she opened a cupboard to get out dinner plates, she asked wearily, "OK. What happened, Jess?"

"Well . . ." Jessica started slicing the tomato, her eyes narrowed in concentration. "You know Jack Hunter is giving a concert here soon, and A.J. wasn't able to get tickets."

Jack Hunter, a hot new rock star, was coming to Sweet Valley in a few weeks. Tickets had gone on sale nearly a month ago and had sold out instantly.

"Anyway," Jessica continued, "Lila's dad can get two tickets for Lila, and she said she'd take me, but that would mean that A.J. wouldn't get to go, and I don't think he'll like being left out."

"That's too bad." Opening a drawer, Elizabeth grabbed forks and knives. She shrugged. "Maybe you shouldn't go."

"There's no way I'm not going," Jessica replied emphatically. "But A.J. will probably act all hurt and rejected."

"True."

Jessica glared at Elizabeth. "You're not being a lot of help, you know."

"Well, what do you expect me to say?" Elizabeth snapped. She was surprised at her hostility, but she just wasn't in the mood to listen to Jessica's petty problems. With what she had been through at the hospital, rock concerts seemed pretty trivial.

Seeing the surprised look in her twin's eyes, however, Elizabeth softened her tone. "Look, Jess, I'm really tired, and it honestly doesn't matter very much to me how you work out this crisis, OK?"

Jessica pouted. "You don't have to bite my head off, you know."

"I'm sorry I yelled. Just don't expect me to

solve every problem that comes along, that's all." As she spoke Elizabeth realized she was being defensive because of what had happened with John. He had turned to her for advice, and now things were in worse shape than before.

So now I'm taking it out on Jess. Shaking her head, she stepped over to her twin and hugged her impulsively. "I'm in a bad mood. Just forget it."

An hour later both Mr. and Mrs. Wakefield had come home, and the family sat down to dinner. As he served the lasagna, Ned Wakefield gave Elizabeth an inquisitive look. "You're pretty quiet tonight, Liz. What's up?"

Elizabeth toyed with her water glass. "You know Mr. Mitchell?"

"Sure. He's with Wells and Wells. I heard he's in the hospital," Mr. Wakefield added. "Doesn't he have a daughter in your class?"

"She's a *sophomore*," Jessica supplied in a superior tone.

Elizabeth glanced at her sister but didn't comment. Instead, she turned back to her father. "I was over at the hospital with her—her name's Jennifer—this afternoon and he had just gone in for a heart bypass—"

"Oh, no!" Mrs. Wakefield gasped. She looked at her husband with concern. "It must be a rough time for them. I hope everything goes all right."

Mr. Wakefield looked thoughtful. "The surgeons at Fowler Memorial are excellent, Alice. He's still a young man. He should do fine." His gaze rested on Elizabeth for a moment, and he registered the anxious look on her face. "How about if I make a call tomorrow over to Wells and Wells? They'll probably have some news."

Elizabeth smiled gratefully. All things considered, John probably wouldn't be hearing from Jennifer. And Elizabeth knew that if she had anything to tell him the next day, he would appreciate it. "Thanks, Dad," she replied. "That'd be great."

Eleven

When Elizabeth got to school on Thursday morning, she found Enid Rollins waiting for her by their lockers.

"Liz! Thank goodness you're here!"

Elizabeth greeted her best friend with a broad grin. "It's nice to feel wanted," she said. As she began to turn her combination lock, she prompted, "So what's up? You look excited."

"I need your help with something really important," Enid explained. "The Big Sisters program has been recruiting at my mother's office, and Mom and I were talking about it. We thought it'd be great if we could get girls from school to be Big Sisters, too."

Elizabeth paused with her hand inside her locker and stared in admiration at Enid. Sometimes it seemed her best friend had the biggest heart of anyone she knew. Enid was always doing things for other people, and that was one reason why Elizabeth loved her so much.

"That's a great idea," Elizabeth said. She hurriedly pulled out her chemistry book. "I'm not sure I have the time, though, with everything else I'm doing. What would we have to do?"

"Well, basically, match up motherless, underprivileged girls with girls at school who have similar interests or backgrounds. Just coordinate the whole thing, really."

Nodding, Elizabeth shut her locker, and they started walking toward their homerooms through the noisy, crowded hallway. The more she thought about it, the more Elizabeth liked it. There were plenty of juniors and seniors who could really make a difference in little girls' lives. Elizabeth knew her older brother, Steven, had made growing up special for her—even if he was a pain at times! Not having an older sibling to turn to for advice and friendship had to be a lonely way to grow up, she thought, especially for an underprivileged child.

"Have you talked to anyone at the Big Sisters office?" Elizabeth asked.

Enid nodded enthusiastically. "Yesterday. And they said they could get a list of at least seven girls to start with."

"Enid, you sneak," Elizabeth looked at her best friend and shook her head.

"What?"

"You never said anything about this, and you've done all this planning already."

Enid shrugged nonchalantly. "Oh, that's just the way we sneaky people do things," she said. Grinning, she grabbed Elizabeth's hand. "So will you help?"

"Of course I will, you dope! I'm busy, but this sounds too good to say no to. When do we start?"

They stopped outside Enid's homeroom, and Enid shifted her books from one arm to the other. "As soon as I get the list, and maybe you could put something in *The Oracle*."

"Good idea," Elizabeth replied warmly. "I can make the deadline this afternoon, and it'll be ready for Monday's paper."

"This is really going to be great, Liz. I'll talk to you later."

"OK. Bye."

As Elizabeth turned to head for her own homeroom, she started to think about the project. Already she could think of half a dozen friends of hers who would probably be willing to participate. With a feeling of enormous satisfaction, she slipped into her homeroom and took her seat.

All morning John tried to catch a glimpse of Jennifer, but without success. He was nearly sick with worry wondering how Mr. Mitchell was doing. His parents had tried getting in touch with Mrs. Mitchell, but there hadn't been any answer at the house, and they didn't want to intrude at the hospital. So John was hoping that even if Jennifer didn't want to talk to him, at least she would tell him if her father was all right. Finally he ran across a girl from Jennifer's homeroom and asked if Jennifer had been in for attendance. When he found out she wasn't in school, he grew even more concerned.

Deeply troubled, he drifted into the cafeteria at lunchtime, even though he didn't have any appetite. He stood still, gazing blankly at nothing and wondering what he should do.

"John, how is everything?"

He sighed gratefully at the sight of Elizabeth. At least there was one person who sympathized with what he was going through. "I don't know. Jennifer isn't in school today, and there's no answer at the Mitchells'. I don't know what to do."

"Did you try calling over at the hospital again?" she asked. She gestured toward a nearby empty table, and they sat down.

John rested his arms on the table and shook his head. He wished he could disappear. Everything was such a mess, and he didn't know how to straighten it all out again. "They won't tell me anything." He sighed. "God, I feel like the biggest jerk in the world. It's all my fault."

"John." Elizabeth spoke in a firm tone and looked at him squarely. "Listen, it's not your fault Mr. Mitchell has a bad heart, and it's not your fault that Rick Andover broke into the music store. You're not responsible for all the bad things that happen in the world."

He managed a weak smile, but he still felt terrible. "I just— What if he died? What if that's why Jennifer isn't in school today? What if—"

"Come on," she interrupted, rising. She led John out into the hallway. When she reached the pay phone, she dug some change out of her purse and started punching in a phone number. "I'm calling my father," she explained. "He can call his friend over at Wells and Wells and find out."

John felt a surge of relief that Elizabeth was on his side. But he waited apprehensively, almost unable to listen to the one-sided conversation.

"Hi, it's Liz Wakefield," Elizabeth said cheerfully. "Is my dad in? Thanks. Hi, Dad. Yeah, did you call yet? OK, I'll wait." She covered up the mouthpiece and looked at John, her blue-green eyes warm with compassion. "He put me on hold so he can call Wells and Wells on another line. It'll just be a minute."

John swallowed hard and nodded. He was afraid the news would be bad. If it was, he didn't know what he would do. Jennifer would never speak to him again. His heart pounding, he leaned against the wall and stared blindly at his sneakers.

"Oh—hi, Dad," Elizabeth said into the phone.

A jolt of adrenaline ran through John when Elizabeth's father came back on the line. He looked at her nervously and then glanced away.

"OK. Sure. That's great. Thanks a lot. See you later, Dad." Smiling, Elizabeth hung up the phone and turned to John. "He made it through just fine. He's back in Intensive Care, but he's already feeling a lot better, they say."

John felt his shoulders sag with relief. He passed one shaking hand across his forehead and nodded. "That's great. Oh, man. I was so—"

"It's OK," Elizabeth cut in. She gave him a sympathetic smile. "You can stop blaming yourself now. He's going to be fine."

"Right." John looked off down the hallway, a hundred thoughts rushing through his head. But the most important one was: *How is Jennifer taking it?*

Of course she would be relieved, but she must still be under an enormous strain. There was a long convalescence to get through, and after all, Mr. Mitchell was still in Intensive Care. The ordeal wasn't over yet.

"It's probably a good time for you to talk to Jennifer," Elizabeth said, interrupting his thoughts. "Now that her father's going to be all right, she's probably a lot less upset."

"I wouldn't count on it," John said. "She's not going to just forget about what I did."

Elizabeth shrugged. "No. But you can at least give it a shot. You two had a good friendship. Go see if it's still there."

"I can't." Panicked, John backed up. "Can't *you* go? Just to see how she is? Please?"

"John—" Elizabeth let out a sharp, exasperated sigh. Then she said, "All right, look. After school we can both go to the hospital, and I'll go in and see how Jennifer is. If she feels like talking to you, then you'll be there, and you can go in."

He hesitated, but he had to admit it was a sensible plan. And besides, he had asked a lot from Elizabeth lately, and she had helped him without complaint. It was no time to start acting like a whiny kid.

"OK. And thanks, Liz. You're a really great person."

Elizabeth's dimple showed in her left cheek as she grinned modestly. "I bet you say that to everyone," she teased.

"No, just you." John felt better than he had in days. Things might still be up in the air, but he knew he had a lot going for him. And Elizabeth Wakefield was one of them. He punched her playfully in the shoulder. "See you after school."

Elizabeth put the Fiat in gear and backed out of her parking space, then swung around into the main driveway to the school entrance. She waited there while students streamed out of the building and down the wide marble steps. Friends called to her as they passed, and she waved in return. Her eyes were on the big double doors, though, while she scanned the crowd for John Pfeifer. When he appeared at the top of the steps, he saw her and trotted down.

"Hi," he said, clambering in. His face was flushed, and he didn't seem to know where to put his arms and legs. He kept shifting around awkwardly in the seat.

Elizabeth resisted the impulse to smile. She realized he was nervous about confronting Jennifer, and she didn't want to make it any worse. With a faint, sympathetic grin, she started up the car and pulled away from the curb.

"I called her house again," John said abruptly. "There's still no one home, so I figure they're still at the hospital."

"OK."

"And I was also thinking about what you could say," John went on. He stretched his neck and then shrugged uncomfortably. "You could ask her—"

Elizabeth shot a look at him. "John, don't worry. I'll just play it by ear."

They drove in silence until the hospital loomed before them.

"I was thinking—maybe I should wait a few days, just let things settle down," John mumbled, obviously dreading Jennifer's reaction.

Elizabeth shrugged. "OK, if that's the way you want it. But we're here. I think I'll go in anyway, just to say hello. You can wait outside if you want." She glanced at him from the corner of her eye and then looked ahead again. Inwardly, she believed the best time for him to talk to Jennifer was now. The sooner the better.

But there was no harm in her scouting out the territory first, Elizabeth knew. So she didn't argue with John. Instead, she found a parking space and cut the engine. They sat looking at each other for a moment.

"So . . . I'll be back in a few minutes," she said.

John nodded, trying to stay composed. "I'll be here."

Without another word, Elizabeth climbed out, swung her bag over her shoulder, and headed for the main visitors' entrance. Inside the cool, hushed lobby, she paused. An idea came to her. At one time she had worked in the hospital as a candy striper, so she knew the place well. Turning to the right, she hurried down a hallway in the direction of a florist shop.

"Hello," she called to the white-haired woman

at the counter. She took her wallet out of her purse and made a hasty calculation. "What do you have for twelve dollars?" she asked.

The saleswoman beamed. "Visiting someone in your family, dear?"

"No, just a friend."

"Well, that's nice. It's nice to see young people come visiting. Let me see . . ." Sliding open the glass refrigerator door, the woman lifted out a small arrangement of white carnations and yellow daisies. "This one is only eleven dollars. Plus tax."

Elizabeth nodded, pleased with the simple bouquet. "That's fine."

"And I'll put a bow on it, dear. And here's our selection of note cards, too. Just fill one out while I ring this up."

Her eyes sparkling, Elizabeth chose a card with a red rose on it, picked up a pen, and paused for a moment to consider. Then she carefully wrote a few lines and signed it. After she paid for the flowers, Elizabeth hurried to the elevator, crossed her fingers, and pressed the button.

Twelve

Mr. Mitchell stirred slightly in his bed and sighed. He was deeply sedated. Jennifer looked across the bed at her mother. Their eyes met, and they exchanged faint, hopeful smiles.

"I think I'll go get something to eat, Jen," Mrs. Mitchell said in a quiet voice. She stood up and stretched. "Why don't you come with me? Dad won't be waking up for a while."

But Jennifer shook her head. "No, you go ahead, Mom. I'm not really hungry right now. I'll just stay here with him."

Her mother looked at her for a moment, then smiled tenderly. "OK, honey. I won't be more than a few minutes."

"Sure. Take your time." Jennifer watched as her mother left the dimly lit hospital room, and then she relaxed against the chair. A shaft of afternoon sunlight sliced through the crack between the shade and the window.

Jennifer studied her father's face in the gentle light. He looked peaceful, and his breathing was deep and regular. A faint echo of the pain he had felt tugged at her own heart as she looked at him.

"I'm sorry, Dad. I'll make it up to you," she whispered. "I really will."

She wanted to touch his hand, but she was afraid to disturb him. When she thought of the awful way she had treated him, how she had turned her back on him when he was in such pain, tears pricked her eyelids.

I love you, Dad, she told him silently. *You know that, don't you?*

Sighing, she stood up and slipped out into the hallway to stretch her legs. As she shut the door behind her she heard someone call her name. She looked up anxiously, expecting a nurse or an orderly. Instead, Elizabeth Wakefield was walking toward her, a flower arrangement in her hands. For a moment Jennifer was too surprised to say anything. Until the day before, she had assumed Elizabeth didn't even know who she was. And now she had come to see her in the hospital.

"Hi, Jennifer. How's your dad?" Elizabeth asked quietly, reaching her side. She glanced at the door. "Will he be all right?"

Jennifer nodded.

"I found these flowers at the nurses' station,"

Elizabeth explained. She held out the arrangement of carnations and daisies and nodded back down the hall. "I hope you don't mind that I brought them."

"No—no. It's OK," Jennifer answered without emotion.

"There's a card, too. I'll hold the flowers while you read it."

Jennifer took the card out of the arrangement and carefully slipped the tiny card out of its envelope. She read it aloud.

" 'Dear Mr. and Mrs. Mitchell and Jennifer, I wish you all the best, and my thoughts are with you. I hope you'll always think of me as your friend. Love, John Pfeifer.' "

Jennifer took the arrangement out of Elizabeth's hands and started to walk toward a nearby trash bin. "I don't want these," she said in a tight voice. "He has no right to—"

"Don't throw them away," Elizabeth cut in. She gently took the flowers from Jennifer. "I'm sure he's only trying to help, to be your friend."

Jennifer turned on her heels and stalked indignantly down the corridor, Elizabeth following close behind. When she got to the lounge, Jennifer sank down on a couch and caught her breath. Her heart was pounding wildly in her chest, and her throat felt tight. As she squeezed her hands together, she realized she was still holding the note. She stared at it and at the signature: "Love, John Pfeifer."

Suddenly she was crying, the tears running uncontrollably down her face. Elizabeth reached for her hand and held it without speaking, and Jennifer let the tears flow. She didn't know why she was crying, why her heart felt as though it were splitting in two. All she knew was that she had to cry. Finally, after a few minutes, her sobs eased off into hiccups and sniffles, and she wiped futilely at her wet cheeks.

"I don't know what's wrong with me," she choked, catching her breath. "My dad's fine now."

"It's probably just a release—the relief," Elizabeth offered. There was a box of tissues nearby, and Elizabeth plucked two from the box to give to Jennifer. "It's perfectly natural."

"I guess." Jennifer sniffled. "The past few days have been really tense."

Elizabeth smiled. "I know. But it's all over now. Things are starting to shape up."

They were silent for a few awkward seconds. Jennifer gazed forlornly at the note she still held in her hands and shook her head from side to side.

"John . . ." The name came out as a sigh. Jennifer leaned back and closed her eyes, trying to come to grips with the wild swirl of thoughts and emotions inside her. When she started to talk, she almost felt as if it were another person speaking.

"When he told me he was the one who called the police, I thought I hated him so much. I really did. I'd trusted him, I'd told him everything, and then he went and spied on Rick and turned him in."

Elizabeth didn't say anything, but she nodded.

"But, you know, when my dad was in the operating room, I was thinking about how I'd told him I hated him, and suddenly I didn't want to hate anyone anymore. Especially not John."

"He didn't want to see you get hurt," Elizabeth said. "He was just so worried about you."

Jennifer thought back to the days when she had been so crazy about Rick Andover. It seemed like years ago. Now that she had been separated from him, she realized that what she had felt had been just a wild infatuation. It was even getting hard for her to picture his face clearly.

And now that she faced the truth, she knew Rick really had broken into the music store, and she had to accept that her father had had good cause to give her all those warnings: Rick was trouble, and if it hadn't been for John, she would have been right in the middle of it. Obviously John had recognized that all along. No wonder he had been worried about her.

"He probably thought I was crazy for saying my dad framed Rick," Jennifer said, sniffling.

"I mean, I knew Rick had been found with the guitar and the money, but for some reason I just didn't want to believe he could have stolen them. I—I just wanted to blame somebody else besides Rick."

Elizabeth nodded, and Jennifer let her breath out slowly. "And if John hadn't turned Rick in, I wouldn't have been here with my dad when he—" Her throat constricted without warning. She had to swallow hard to compose herself.

"But you *were* here. That's what matters," Elizabeth finished for her. She leaned forward and squeezed Jennifer's hand. "And when your father wakes up, he'll see you, and he'll probably jump right out of bed, he'll be so happy."

Jennifer let out a combination laugh and hiccup, and she wiped her nose again with her crumpled tissues. "Yeah."

"And you know," Elizabeth went on gently, "John wanted to give you that chance. He could have gone on letting you think your dad was to blame, but he's just not like that."

"I know. I know it," Jennifer whispered. She pressed her lips together. Her eyes felt hot, but she knew she was finished crying.

Thinking it all over now, she realized it had taken a lot of guts for John to admit he was the person to blame, especially since he knew how angry and hurt she was. He had been willing to take all the responsibility on himself.

He's the best friend I've ever had, Jennifer thought.

Beside her, Elizabeth shifted on the couch. "Do you think you can forgive him? He's always been there for you," Elizabeth pointed out. "Give him a chance to make it up."

With a quavery smile, Jennifer looked up and nodded. "I know he's always been there for me. I just always took it for granted before."

Elizabeth's eyes shone with happiness. "He's here now, too. I could go get him, if you want."

An unexpected attack of shyness came over Jennifer. "OK," she whispered, dropping her gaze. She fingered the card, and a smile turned up the corners of her mouth. "I should at least tell him how much I like the flowers he sent."

Elizabeth jumped up from the couch with a wide grin. "Great. I'll go tell him to come up. I'll see you later."

As Elizabeth hurried away to the elevator, Jennifer looked down again at the card in her hand.

"I hope you'll always think of me as your friend," it said. Feeling shy and awkward, but happy all the same, Jennifer smiled.

I've been acting like a spoiled brat, she told herself. *It's time to grow up and take a look around.*

And the one person she was ready to take a good look at at the moment was John Pfeifer.

125

*   *   *

After fifteen minutes of waiting, John was beginning to think he'd go out of his mind. He got out of Elizabeth's car and leaned against it, his arms folded across his chest and his legs crossed. He squinted up at the hospital's windows, wondering what was going on inside. There might be a dozen life-and-death dramas unfolding as he stood there, but only one mattered to him.

Drawing a deep breath to steady his nerves, he pushed himself away from the car and began pacing. The rush of elation that had lifted his spirits when he heard Mr. Mitchell was all right had faded. There were still a hundred things that could go wrong.

But even if nothing goes wrong, there's still reason for Jennifer to hate me, he told himself. *I lied to her, I betrayed her trust, and I let her go on hating her father.*

"She's not going to want to see me," he said out loud. He said it again to convince himself, to make himself face reality. "She *won't* want to see me."

A pregnant woman walking from her car gave him a suspicious look, and John turned away in embarrassment, trying to look casual. He was caught off guard when he heard Elizabeth's voice behind him.

"Hi." She was out of breath.

John's heart jumped and started beating hard as he turned to face Elizabeth. He couldn't speak. He was too afraid to ask.

"She's had a chance to think it all over," Elizabeth told him cheerfully. "And she wants to talk to you—and not to chew you out," she added when a look of alarm passed across his face.

Finally he cleared his throat and darted a quick, hopeful glance at the hospital. "Really?"

"Yes," Elizabeth said, chuckling. "Go on up."

John took a few steps and halted, still uncertain. He couldn't believe Jennifer was actually willing to talk to him after what he had done. It was too good to be true.

Elizabeth let out a groan and shoved him from behind. "Go on, silly! Oh, before I forget—"

"What?" He looked back at her, suddenly impatient to leave.

"You owe me eleven dollars and sixty-six cents, but you can pay me back later."

He stared at her in bewilderment. "Huh?"

"And also," Elizabeth added, her eyes dancing with laughter, "you have very good taste in flowers."

John was even more puzzled and confused than before, but he was too excited and happy to care. He shrugged and gave her a skeptical grin. "If you say so, Liz."

"You want me to wait and drive you home?"

John thought for a moment. "I think I'll take the bus. Thanks."

"OK, no problem."

Grinning from ear to ear, Elizabeth climbed into her convertible and started it up. She looked as if she were enjoying some private joke, but John didn't have time to ask what it was. As he jogged toward the hospital entrance, Elizabeth drove past and waved. He waved in return, then ran inside without looking back.

Once inside, he hurried for the elevator and clenched his fists, anxious for it to come. Finally the car arrived, and he stepped in and pushed the correct button. But when he reached the Intensive Care floor and the doors slid open, he suddenly wished it had all taken a little longer. He didn't know what he was going to say.

Swallowing hard, he walked out into the corridor and glanced left and right. At the far end, Jennifer was sitting on a couch with her back to him. He would recognize the long, straight blond hair anywhere. Beside her on a little table was a bouquet of flowers.

Go on. Just go on and say hi, he commanded himself. His feet seemed to be glued to the floor, but he managed to force himself down the corridor. When he reached her, he cleared his throat. "Hi."

She looked up swiftly, a glow of warmth in her eyes. A tiny smile turned up her lips. "Hi."

They looked at each other for an awkward, silent moment, and then Jennifer broke eye contact. "Thanks for the flowers," she said softly.

"For the—?" Confused, John looked at the flowers, and then he remembered what Elizabeth had said in the parking lot. He grinned and sat down. It was going to be all right. He could feel it. "No problem," he said with a soft chuckle. "How's your father?"

"Good. He's OK." Jennifer nodded and looked up at him again. The happiness in her eyes was beautiful to John. "So are you."

They smiled shyly at each other again. Tipping his head to one side, John asked, "Do you want to go down to the cafeteria? I could get you a Coke or something."

"Sure," Jennifer replied. She picked up the flower arrangement and stood up. "Let's go."

Thirteen

When Elizabeth got home, she went into the kitchen to pour herself a tall glass of orange juice. As she stood at the table drinking, the sound of muffled laughter reached her ears. She walked into the dining room and glanced out the sliding glass doors. Jessica and A.J. were sitting at the patio table together, doing homework.

Curious, Elizabeth watched them for a moment. A.J. leaned close to Jessica and whispered something that sent her into gales of laughter, and then Jessica reached out to caress A.J.'s arm. To Elizabeth, they looked like a completely different pair than they had looked recently. Jessica's eyes glowed with happiness, and A.J. couldn't stop looking at her. If there was ever an example of a couple in love, Jessica and A.J. were it.

Even though Elizabeth didn't want to spy on them, she couldn't help being intrigued. She wondered what could have happened to produce such a dramatic change. Instead of pouting, Jessica was smiling; instead of looking anxious, A.J. looked captivated. And knowing her twin the way she did, Elizabeth knew there was a good chance Jessica had manipulated the situation in an underhanded way. But there could be a different reason, too, she decided fairly. Puzzled, Elizabeth slid open the door.

"Hi, you guys!"

They turned around with a blank, surprised expression, as though they had forgotten there were other people on the planet. "Oh, hi, Lizzie," Jessica called back. She faced A.J. again.

Elizabeth sighed and leaned against the doorframe for a minute, just relaxing and letting her mind wander. Jessica's voice reached her ears clearly.

"Well, anyway, I just felt so bad for all those poor little girls. I knew we had to do something."

"I think it's great you got Liz and Enid to help out with the plan," A.J. said admiringly.

The meaning of their words slowly sank in, and Elizabeth stared at her twin in disbelief. As usual, Jessica was taking the credit for something—this time, for starting up the Big Sisters program at school. Just then, Jessica glanced her way and caught Elizabeth's skeptical expression.

Jessica jumped up, her jaw set. She hurried toward Elizabeth and brushed past her into the house.

"Why are you looking at me that way?"

"I don't know what you're talking about," Elizabeth replied. She took another sip of juice.

Jessica stood near the door with her hands on her hips. "You were giving me this *look*," she said peevishly. She glanced back out at the patio again.

Sighing, Elizabeth put her glass down on the dining room table. "Sorry. Whatever the look was, I didn't mean it. I was just surprised to see you and A.J. getting along so well, that's all. It seemed like you two had been arguing a lot lately."

"What are you talking about?" Jessica demanded. She looked appalled at the thought. "We never argue. And we're getting along fine. Never better."

"Yes, I can see that. But what changed things?"

Jessica wrinkled her brow and shook her head. "I don't know what you mean, Liz. Nothing's changed. I'm just in love, if you know what I mean."

"And so is A.J., I guess." Elizabeth looked out at A.J. again and shrugged. "I guess I'm just imagining things, Jess. Sorry."

Jessica nodded and ran back outside again.

I must have made too big a deal out of their differences, Elizabeth mused. *Maybe they know how to work things out, after all.*

She felt a little chagrined at not giving her sister more credit. All along Elizabeth had assumed that the differences between Jessica and A.J. were just too big to ignore, but maybe they weren't. Besides, every couple ran into rough times together and survived. Certainly she and Jeffrey had. So there was no reason to think Jessica and A.J.'s relationship wouldn't make it.

But if Jessica patched things up by telling lies to make A.J. admire her, what kind of relationship was that? Elizabeth shook her head slowly. With that kind of deception, how long *could* Jessica's romance with A.J. last?

Immediately after school on Friday, a big group of juniors and seniors congregated in the school parking lot. A holiday mood was in the air, and Elizabeth felt herself smiling broadly.

"Another weekend," she said as Jeffrey draped one arm across her shoulders. "Hurray!"

He pulled her close and wiggled his eyebrows up and down. "We'd better do something to be thankful about, huh?"

She giggled and bumped him with her hip. Everyone in the crowd was laughing and talking, exchanging weekend plans. Jessica and A.J. were in the center of one group, which suddenly let out a round of applause. Bruce Patman held up his hands as though he were accepting it.

Shouting for quiet, Ken Matthews and Winston Egbert donned sunglasses and climbed up on top of Winston's battered Volkswagen. They were both wearing flowered Bermuda shorts and mismatched Hawaiian-print shirts.

Ken whistled shrilly through two fingers. "OK, listen up, all you lowly peons!" he called out. He gestured to Winston and bowed from the waist.

With a modest smile, Winston acknowledged the boos and catcalls and applause from his audience.

"Nice legs, Win," Cara said, giggling.

"Thank you." Winston's long skinny legs looked like two poles sticking out of dirty white hightops. "As you all know," he began in an oratorical style, "it's Friday afternoon once again." There was more applause and whistling. "And once again, it is time to *hit the beach!*"

"Ow!" crowed Aaron Dallas.

Another round of applause swept the crowd, and Lila shouted, "Time to party!"

Elizabeth grinned as she surveyed the scene. It never ceased to amaze her how much energy her friends had. Every weekend was a whole new cause for celebration. The tennis courts at the end of the parking lot were virtually empty. It seemed that practically no one stayed at school on Friday afternoons. Most people wanted to get as early a start on the weekend as possible.

Except for one person. On one of the courts, Kristin Thompson was practicing her serve by herself. Elizabeth felt a pang of sympathy for her, and she looked up at Jeffrey.

"I think I'll ask Kristin if she wants to go to the beach with us. It might be a change from practicing all the time."

"Good idea."

Smiling, Elizabeth detached herself from the group and jogged to the fence. "Hi, Kristin?"

Kristin turned, her tennis racket still poised. "Oh, hi, Jessica."

"I'm Elizabeth, Jessica's twin," Elizabeth corrected her with a laugh. She nodded toward the group of students. "We're all going to the beach, and I was wondering if you wanted to come along."

Kristin smiled. "Thanks, but I'm meeting my coach at the club in a few minutes. She's getting there late today, so I thought I'd just hit a few balls here before I meet her."

"But it's Friday!" Elizabeth said in a cajoling tone. She wanted Kristin to feel welcome. She turned as Bruce Patman joined her at the fence. "Tell her, Bruce. It's too hot to play tennis."

Bruce gave Kristin an appraising glance. "She's right. Besides, these courts are supposed to be closed on Friday afternoons. Didn't anyone tell you?"

"No—I—" A look of dismay crossed Kristin's face.

"He's just kidding," Elizabeth said quickly. "But we'd really like you to come. Honest."

"Yeah," Bruce drawled. His eyes ran over Kristin again while a slow, seductive smile turned up one corner of his mouth.

"Come on—come to the beach, and we can get something to eat afterward," he invited, twining his fingers in the chain-link fence.

Kristin smiled back at Bruce, and her cheeks turned slightly pink. But she continued to shake her head. "Sorry, I have to go to my tennis lesson. Thanks for asking, though."

"You're sure?"

"Positive."

Shrugging, Bruce took a step backward. "Some other time," he said.

Elizabeth thought Bruce looked a bit irritated. He wasn't used to being refused point-blank, and she couldn't help feeling a little bit smug about it. Bruce was so arrogant that his ego needed periodic deflating. Being turned down by a pretty girl once in a while wouldn't kill him.

As they both turned to head back for the group, Elizabeth cast one last look back at Kristin. She had heard Kristin was a dedicated tennis player, and that certainly seemed to be the case. Elizabeth wondered if there was any way at all to tempt Kristin to do something other then play tennis. If she wouldn't go to the beach on a blistering hot Friday, she probably wouldn't do anything else!

Is Elizabeth right? Is it true there's nothing that will tear Kristin away from the tennis court? Find out in Sweet Valley High #53, SECOND CHANCE.

YOUR OWN

SLAM BOOK!

If you've read *Slambook Fever*, Sweet Valley High #48, you know that slam books are the rage at Sweet Valley High. Now *you* can have a slam book of your own! Make up your own categories, such as "Biggest Jock" or "Best Looking," and have your friends fill in the rest! There's a four-page calendar, horoscopes and questions most asked by Sweet Valley readers with answers from Elizabeth and Jessica

It's a must for SWEET VALLEY fans!

☐ 05496- **FRANCINE PASCAL'S SWEET VALLEY HIGH SLAM BOOK**
 Laurie Pascal Wenk   **$3.95**
